I0763468

DEATH AT HELICON HEIGHTS

 This is a work of fiction, and the characters, setting, and events do not reference any actual past or present persons, situations, or events.

Printed in the United States of America

First Printing 2024

ISBN Hardback: 978-1-7357825-7-7

ISBN Paperback: 978-1-7357825-3-9

Contents

DEATH AT HELICON HEIGHTS

PREFACE

Ambiguities in life are often the core of fiction, engaging the chords of experiences we have had, but with nuances that add interest, invite expectations, and proceed to resolutions that confound the threads of our imagination. There are also ambiguities regarding death: was it inevitable, could it have been prevented, was someone at fault, how great was the loss to the living?

This novel, the fourth of the author's Ted Born Classic Courtroom Trials series, follows talented Constance Stanfield, young mother of two beautiful children, in her effort to expand the appreciation of beautiful lace, and delicate hand sewing within her community and beyond. Steeped in her love of ancient Greek culture, Constance and her husband Jeremy lived in a Greek Revival columned home that she called Helicon Heights, commemorating Mt. Helicon in Greece, where the winged horse Pegasus touched down and caused springs of water to gush up, which the Muses regarded as sacred - Muses who shared their love of beauty with humanity.

Constance joined with a crucially important associate to set up her lace boutique, who shortly afterward abruptly abandoned the deal after Constance has sunk a lot of borrowed money into it. After much resistance to explaining why she abandoned Constance, the associate revealed an unexpected and off-the-charts reason for her abrupt departure. Constance hired attorney Ted Born to sue her former associate for damages; the lawsuit was successful but did not fully compensate Constance for her damages. Thus, crippled financially from the beginning and lacking the personal participation of her former key associate, Constance's enterprise failed to achieve its goals, and the financial situation was getting progressively worse. Constance's husband was not supportive of her during her difficult times, going from indifference, to worse. Constance needed to rely on Ted Born's advice regarding a number of issues as she continued on. At one point, Constance tried to salvage her business through an arrangement with another startup venture featuring synthetic or simulated lace, but that initiative proved to be of limited help in the long run.

The author lays bare the innermost feelings and thoughts of Constance and the other characters via you-are-there insights provided by dialogue and by verbatim mental reflections. Mostly, there is sympathy for and empathy with Constance, but the legitimate concerns of her husband and others in the narrative are also treated objectively, and their characters become understandable and relatable.

As Constance's circumstances got more desperate, she resorted to a mix of alcohol and pain pills, and finally to unbelievable other measures to deal with her depression, which at times will evoke horror and a variety of strong emotions.

As suggested above, there are ambiguities regarding the death of Constance, whether it was murder, an accident, or suicide.

It will be up to the reader to resolve this ambiguity based on all the events and clues leading up to the demise of Constance. This novel is somewhat different from the author's previous novels, in that the suspenseful climax occurs not in the trial itself, but what comes after the end.

It is a gripping story of good intentions that proved impossible of fulfillment, resulting in frustration and lost talent. The reader is left to decide the ambiguity in Constance's death, sifting all the information provided: was it was suicide, accident or murder?

CHAPTER ONE:
The Phone Call

Ted Born turned over in bed and looked at the alarm clock. It was Sunday morning, and Ted had no professional obligations at his law office that day, but he had planned to go to early church. He looked toward his wife Lydia who seemed to be still asleep. There was no sound from the rooms of their two children. He hoped Lydia could sleep a few more minutes while he went to the shower and began shaving, but he knew she would soon be rousing herself.

He looked out a bathroom window on a sky morphing from gray to light blue. "It looks like this is going to be a gorgeous day," he said to himself. By the time he got out of the shower, the gray sky had become bluer, and the pink and gold flourishes were nearly gone. "Things change. Sunrises come and go, but the blue sky is a nice backdrop, and it will stay longer. It's the natural order of things. All's right with the world."

Lydia had gotten up and was checking on the children, as he began shaving. Just as he was finishing, Lydia knocked on the bathroom door and came in. "Ted, I don't know what's wrong with me. I just feel something isn't right. It's not that I feel physically ill; it's just an uneasiness I can't put my finger on."

"What could be wrong, Lydia? We're both healthy. We have two great kids. And it looks like a beautiful day ahead. I don't even have to go to the office, and I am going to take you and the children out to brunch today after church. Cheer up," Ted tried to assure her.

Ted and Lydia sat down to breakfast and were shortly joined by the children who were only partially dressed. Lydia said to the children, "I suppose I'm old-fashioned. I like for you to come to the table dressed, but in the interest of time, come on and join us. But right after breakfast go back to your rooms and get dressed so we can go to church." Cranberry muffins, orange juice, a small compote of strawberries and blueberries, and tea and coffee were on the table, except the children had tall glasses of milk.

Their daughter Rebecca looked at Ted and asked, "Daddy, tell me what it's like to be a lawyer."

"Well, Rebecca, that could take a while, but basically, we have customers - we call them 'clients' - and they have different kinds of problems that somehow involve our laws, or sometimes they are just afraid they might run into problems later, and they want to find a legal way to avoid them. Sometimes they have disputes with other people that are so serious they can't work them out, and they have to go to Court where a Judge, and often a jury, has to solve their problems for them. We lawyers are trained in the law, of course, and we have had a lot of experience dealing with different kinds of problems, so we are there to advise them and stand by them as they try to work through their problems, or we take charge of their case in the courtroom. That's it in a nutshell. As lawyers, we try not to let ourselves get too personally emotionally involved in the clients' problems. But I must confess that sometimes I can't help but feel that I am invested in my clients' struggles: That means I feel like my clients' hurts are my hurts, and I want justice for them, really badly," Ted tried to explain.

"Do you have clients like that right now, someone you feel for very much, and you have a hard time helping them?" Rebecca asked.

"Actually, I have several, but there is one in particular that has been on my mind a lot lately. I don't think I should say any more about it. Anyway, we need to finish getting ready for church," Ted said, looking at his watch.

Ted left the table and went to brush his teeth, and he heard the telephone ring. Lydia answered the phone, and he could hear her say, "We're all just about ready to walk out the door. Is it urgent? . . . Oh, NO! I just can't believe that! Hold on and I'll get Ted." Ted had finished brushing his teeth, and Lydia brought the portable phone to him as he emerged from the bathroom. "Ted, it's Marcie, Constance Stanfield's assistant, and something terrible has happened. Here's the phone."

Ted picked up the telephone and heard Marcie sobbing. "Ted, a horrible thing has happened to Constance, and I don't think there's any way you can help her now. I just got a call from her husband Jeremy that he found her dead in her bed this morning! We don't know what happened. He says he doesn't know, that she just went to bed and never woke up. He was very matter of fact about it, controlling his emotions. She depended so much on you, I know you will want to get over to the house and check everything out."

"Marcie, this has hit me like a ton of bricks," Ted said. "I just had some long and very personal conversations with her last week, and we actually prepared, and she executed, a new will last Thursday, and now she's dead? I just can't imagine it, although I must say I've been worried. I'll get Lydia to go ahead and go with the children to church, and I will come right over now." Lydia had been standing beside him as he spoke to Marcie. He handed the phone back to her and said, "The psychic's nightmare has happened. God help us!"

CHAPTER TWO:
In the Beginning

It had all begun about three years earlier, when Constance Stanfield had developed a love for lace and beautiful hand sewing.

Constance, with large sewing bag in hand, breathlessly opened the door of the host home, where this week's sewing class was convening, her eyes scanning the large living room filled with other ladies with sewing bags. One of them, Kate Lord, the teacher, was standing in front of a marble fireplace, not in use, and was explaining and answering questions about sewing. She looked up and greeted Constance, "Hi, Connie! Come on in. You may sometimes be late, but we can always count on the fact that you have done your homework. We've been looking at the progress the group has made in sewing lacy children's clothes. I'll bet you have something to show us."

Constance took a seat and said, "Yes, I do, Kate. Sorry I'm late, but you are right. I always try do my homework, because this is fascinating, creative stuff, and I have been working hard to follow the pattern for this outfit for my daughter, Angela. Here's where I am right now. I'm having a little trouble with the lace around the sleeves. I know it can't be too tight or too loose, and I'm having trouble getting it just right. I've undone the stitching twice already. So far, the rest of it seems to be coming along fine," Constance said, proudly holding up her work-in-progress.

“Let’s see if I can help,” Kate said, walking over to Constance’s chair and taking a look at the handiwork. “Okay, here’s what I would do,” picking up the unfinished dress, inspecting it, then giving Constance some pointers. “You are on track to making a stunning dress for Angela.” Then Kate went around the room giving help to each of the ladies, occasionally going back to her central position in front of the fireplace, and making general remarks to the group, based on her observations of problems she had observed.

This was a weekly class the ladies, all with very young children, had signed up for, to learn the fine art of making lacy children’s clothes, mainly for little girls but some for little boys as well. Some of the ladies had been taking classes from Kate, with her individualized hands-on instruction and oversight, for years, off and on, and others were neophytes who wanted to learn. Constance had been taking the classes for a few months, but this lace project had struck a chord in her artistic psyche that was intense - nothing casual about it with Constance. Where others might have viewed the sewing as tedious work, Constance joyfully embraced it as an exciting creative challenge. Kate viewed her as an exemplary student, a kind of lace soulmate.

The group was dependent on Kate not only for instruction, but for acquiring the dress materials and especially the just-right kinds of lace, and sometimes there were delays getting the materials. Then there was the problem of the patterns. Few of the ladies could just conceive a design, size it, and then sew it to finished perfection. Kate had some of her own patterns and knew where to get others.

Constance began wondering why there was not some shop locally that would carry the lace and at least some of the other items so that they would be readily accessible, and perhaps offer access to advice and lessons. She was excited and engrossed in this new world of creativity and beauty, and felt that, surely, there would be many others who would feel likewise if exposed to the art of fine sewing with lace.

Constance found herself alone with Kate at the end of one of the sessions and brought up an idea she had. "Kate, as you have probably gathered, I am quite taken with lace and fine sewing. You are doing a great job with a relatively small group of young mothers. But you are essentially working out of your home, and we meet at various homes that open up to you, where we have the actual classes. Wouldn't it help you - and everybody - if there was a shop that carried everything needed, and where we could reliably go for help whenever we hit a snag in our sewing. It seems to me it would enlarge the group of those who are interested in this kind of thing and would add a special touch when our children can appropriately appear in beautiful clothes - church, birthday parties, holidays, and other similar occasions. Do you follow me, and is this something feasible?"

"Constance, it would be very nice if we had what you are thinking of, but it takes money to do that, and I don't have that kind of money. You know, I am divorced, and I get some help from my ex-husband, but I have to try to make ends meet as best I can. I have some modest assets I've accumulated and am holding onto for my retirement, but there's no way I could invest in anything like that. I think of you as my star student, at least among my current crop, because you think the way I do, and you have enthusiasm as I do. But I don't know how many Constance Stanfields there are around Greenville, South Carolina, and I do this teaching, and some sewing that I sell to department stores, and I pick up other odd jobs, catering and the like, and that's about all I can do," Kate confided.

"Kate, let me think about this and get back in touch with you, and maybe we can figure out a better way of doing this," Constance said.

"Of course. I'm always open to ideas. Thanks, Connie," said Kate.

When Constance had finished the outfit for daughter Angela, she had an idea that she passed by Kate who seemed happy and enthusiastic about it. Then, she unveiled the idea to her husband, Dr. Jeremy Stanfield, a pediatrician. As she laid it out to Jeremy, "I've decided what I'm going to do, Jeremy. I am going to open a lace shop!" Constance announced.

"You are *what* - opening a shop? You aren't serious? Tell me you aren't serious. You've never done anything like that in your life. What is this all about? I would think you are joking, but you've got that look in your eye. Okay, let me have it. What's going on?" her husband demanded, mostly dismissively, a little worried.

"Here's the deal. We have a fine little boy and a gorgeous, cherubic-looking little girl with blonde hair, blue eyes, and just the right amount of natural curl in her hair. She's beautiful! And, as you know, I have always been proud to show her off, and I got interested in lace, because most people these days don't have the time - or take the time - to dress their children in classic lacy outfits. Well, you know what happened next. I met this woman whose friends call her the 'lace lady.' She works out of her home, carries a stock of different laces, knows just what kind of lace ought to go on dresses for little girls, and what goes at the neck and what goes at the sleeves and at the waist and hem, and so I ended up making this stunning lacy dress for Angela, and she looks like an angel in it, true to her name! You know which one I'm talking about, and you liked it, too. I've taken pictures from every angle. Hardly anybody does this kind of thing anymore, but she is a beautiful standout in that dress, and you should hear the 'oohs' and 'ahhs' when people see her in that dress," Constance began.

"Yeah, I kind of know all that. She's beautiful, all right, but where are you going with this crazy idea you think you have?" Jeremy probed.

"Jeremy, all my friends with small children, especially little girls, after seeing Angela, want to get into lace, a nostalgia thing: it recalls the Victorian era, a time when mothers took the time and made the effort to provide something special for their little girls - and there are a few who want to make Little Lord Fauntleroys out of the young boys too. But it is hard to find the laces you need locally to produce these outfits, and even if you can find the lace, most people don't know what to do with it, to produce the right effect. So, I've talked with the lace lady - her name is Kate Lord, you know - about opening a shop. She says she doesn't have the capital to do it right, and she is not sure the market is broad enough to support the right kind of shop in an upscale area.

"So, I proposed a deal where I would fund the shop, rent the space, decorate it, stock it, insure it, cover the overhead, and take 60% of any profits. She would be a 40% owner but would have no risks. I would just expect her to teach classes and seminars and consult with customers on a regular basis. Mainly, I would like her to be visible, the face of the business. She would not have to be there all the time, just on some reasonable schedule, and we would charge fees for her seminars and individual instruction. She is pretty well known among a core group of her regular customers and their friends, and, to take advantage of that, I'm proposing to name the shop after her: Katherine Lord's Laces. Doesn't that have an upscale sound to it? I think it would be fun. The shop would be a kind of social center for all the young mothers who are 'in the know'," Constance explained.

"I hate to burst your bubble, Connie, but I think the lace lady has a point: not a big enough market for this. Where would the money come from? I'm doing all right as a young pediatrician, but I have student loans and we're living in this Greek-revival mansion we can't really afford. You don't have a job that brings in any money, just a lot of volunteer work that gets us written up in the 'society' pages of the newspaper, but you can't take that to the bank. I think you need to get serious and think this through," Jeremy cautioned.

"Okay. Here's the way I look at it. I'm an only child. I think Daddy will be willing to come to the rescue one more time. He made a huge down-payment so we could get this house. He wants us to be one of the up-and-coming young couples in town. He knows I have an artistic bent, and I think he would be pleased that I incorporated my creative interests in a business that potentially could earn money, at the same time consolidating our social status. I think Daddy would spring for this," Constance opined.

"Well, talk it over with him. Whatever you want to do would be, I guess, something I could live with, as long as you aren't looking to me to finance it and as long as it doesn't monopolize your time. I've got my life, and you've got yours, and everybody thinks we are the perfect couple with the perfect family, and it's a benefit to us that they think that. If your dad asks for my input, I guess I'll go along. I know he has a pretty good wad of inherited money; he didn't make all that as a college professor. So, go talk with him and see what he will do, if you are determined. But I won't shed any tears if he turns you down," Jeremy concluded.

CHAPTER THREE:
A Visit with Dad

Constance approached her dad, Professor Grantham Selsby, to plead her case. In his eyes, his daughter was everything a father could hope for - beautiful, bright, talented, married with two fine children, and well accepted socially with lots of friends. He had enjoyed being a college professor, loving the academic atmosphere, the ability to think and write and travel during the summers, especially cruises, protected by a nest-egg inherited from his corporate executive father who had been in the right place at the right time. He had been a stockholder executive in a large company bought out in a deal that provided him with a bundle of money. It had not made him rich at the time, but he invested in the stock market, and he had grown his holdings substantially with successful stock plays. The professor's life and future had turned to Constance after the loss of his wife to a terrible disease a few years earlier. Dr. Selsby was a dapper man in his early 70s, who had lived well, but appeared never to have been self-indulgent, except that he did like cruises. He still enjoyed the company of women his age but had never seemed serious about any of them.

Constance found her father sitting in his favorite well-worn chair in his den, smoking a pipe that he dubiously considered to be a safer alternative to cigarettes. He had an open-neck shirt and somewhat baggy trousers that accommodated his slightly overweight frame, consistent with his professorial profile. On hearing Constance's presentation, the professor said, "Constance,

I don't know anything about lace, and I've never run a business, so I'm not in a good position either to cheer you on or rein in your enthusiasm. I have some experience in investing, and this would not be something that would excite me as an investment bonanza. But I know you are smart, and you seem to know what you are doing and have thought it through. I'll fund this if the figures look reasonable. I just want you to get some good legal advice before you get into this. You will need to form a corporation, protect your 'business franchise' as much as you can, and get yourself a good CPA who can advise you about the finances. Nail down everything about your relationship with the lace lady, Kate Lord. Get me some figures and, if they look reasonable, I will issue checks as needed to cover expenses as you request them. Some of this can be a gift, but for tax reasons some of it will have to be made in the form of a loan, but - don't worry - I will forgive parts of the indebtedness over a period of years to avoid or minimize gift taxes, assuming I can afford it" Selsby promised.

"Any suggestions of a lawyer, Daddy?" Constance asked.

"I hear good things about Ted Born. I don't know him personally, but he's an up-and-coming younger lawyer who seems to know his business. I think he has expertise on setting up corporations and protecting their names and logos, and he also is a fine litigator, if you should ever have to go to Court," Selsby suggested.

"All right. Unless I get some other great suggestions, I will consult with Mr. Born. Thanks, Daddy. I hope I can make you proud of me," said Constance as she got up to leave, planting a parting kiss on her father's forehead.

CHAPTER FOUR:
Making it Happen

Constance had gone to college - some said it was more of a young ladies' "finishing school" - and had spent a year abroad in Italy studying and traveling. She had come to admire the Greek temples planted in the south of Italy by ancient Greek colonizers in places like Paestum, down south near the "ankle" of Italy's boot, inspiring her to travel around in Greece itself. She had an eye for beautiful architecture. She developed a love of travel and, after her marriage to Jeremy, the two of them had embarked on some selective cultural travel, mainly to Europe, at least once traversing the Atlantic on the Concorde. She loved Medieval and Renaissance cathedrals, but the stateliness of the simple Doric columned Greek temples and buildings remained her favorite classical style.

The Stanfields also did a lot of entertaining, and often found themselves mentioned in the society section of the newspaper as one of the "snappiest" couples around. Constance had taken flower arranging classes from a well-known local who had developed a reputation for gorgeous floral arrangements, the kind of thing seen at the most elegant weddings and social events, a cut above the output of typical florist shops, and she loved creating beautiful floral arrangements for her home. Indeed, she had always dreamed of a mansion large enough and fine enough to show off her dramatic floral creations.

Constance had always admired a particular magnificent home, built somewhat in the Greek Revival style, located just outside her hometown of Greenville, South Carolina. It was built on the top of a high hill, with a private road leading up to it. The owner had given it the name Mount Helicon after the real Greek mountain of that name, much celebrated in Greek mythology, although the Carolina setting was not nearly so high as the mountain in Greece. There were old stables remaining on the property that showed the signs of many years of disuse. When the house went on the market, Constance was obsessed with buying it and won a bidding contest with the aid of her father. Before moving in, Constance upgraded the Doric columns rising from a marble porch all along the front, supporting a wrought iron balcony at the second level - although the balcony feature looked more antebellum than Greek. Still, it was a striking mansion, and it satisfied her dream of one day living in a magnificent Greek-style structure.

Constance also found and bought a large Flemish tapestry with a theme of the Valley of the Greek Muses and displayed it in the living room. She hoped to add a painting or tapestry of Poseidon, the Master of Helicon, if she could find something suitable. The lush garden flowers added to the grandeur of it all. Constance gave a name to the long driveway to the mansion: The Pegasus Trail, honoring the visit of the winged horse of mythology whose hoof struck a rock on Mount Helicon and caused a spring to gush forth. There was indeed a spring of clear cold water on the premises, that comprised 14 acres of otherwise undeveloped land.

When they moved into Helicon Heights, Jeremy asked with a wink, "Connie, am I supposed to wear a toga in this house? That could make things interesting at times, toga parties for the two of us, on demand." Constance smiled but gave him a playful education in return, "Jeremy, togas were Roman garments, not worn by the ancient Greeks. The Greeks, both men and women, wore a lighter rectangular garment, while the togas of the Romans were circular. The Greek garment was called a 'himation'. Most Romans didn't wear togas, either, because they were hard to weave, hard to wear properly, and were too hot in summer and not warm enough in winter. Togas became a kind of formal wear used mainly by the Roman upper classes at certain times and places. For a time, I think togas were required to be worn in the Forum, and in latter times they were sometimes worn in areas of the Roman empire outside Rome. But I won't insist on either togas or himations here!"

True to her pledge to herself, Constance did not neglect her flower arranging, but her attention outside the house had now turned more to lace, learning from her mentor, Kate Lord, as she began to plan for her exclusive lace shop her father had promised to back. A suitable location was found for a boutique shop in an upscale area of Greenville, and she and her new partner Kate Lord looked it over and agreed it had potential for their purpose. But first, there was the paperwork - the legal documentation. Constance knew the arrangement between the two of them needed to be in writing, but, despite her father's admonitions, Constance thought she knew the deal well enough and saw no reason to spend the money to get a lawyer involved. So, she wrote something down on a sheet of paper in her own words. It seemed simple. Constance would obtain the lease in her name, pay for the remodeling work to adapt the premises and stock it with lace merchandise, and she and Kate would split the profits on a 60/40 basis, with most of the profit going to Constance. The store would be named after Kate - Katherine Lord's Laces - and Kate would make appearances, give classes and seminars on lace and lacy clothing, and would be available to consult and advise from time to time. They signed a one-page document, and then Kate came over to Helicon Heights for a private celebration, with Champagne, cheese, nuts, and lady fingers. Kate's husband had passed away, so it was just Constance, Jeremy, and Kate at their own private party. However, Kate did not drink alcohol at all, so Jeremy got her a glass of Perrier. Then it turned out that Kate was not fond of cheese, either, and so Constance toasted some saltines with butter on them for Kate. So, Kate had saltines, nuts, and Perrier while the Stanfields had Champagne, nuts, and

Gruyere cheese. However, all of them - Kate included - liked lady fingers. It was a somewhat unusual celebration and did not last long, as Kate needed to get home to feed her cat.

When Kate had left, Jeremy looked at Constance and they both broke into a laugh. "Connie, it looks like you are getting into business with someone you don't know very well! The celebration doesn't seem to auger well for your future relationship," Jeremy teased.

"I can't say that the celebration was a resounding success, maybe flat!" Constance acknowledged, "but cheese and Champagne aren't what is going to determine the success of the business. The woman knows her lace, and she has a good reputation in that area. I have a positive feeling for our project."

The shop area was relatively small. Constance knew she needed to have some space where lace classes could be conducted, and she set aside and furnished an area in the back of the shop for that purpose. Otherwise, she mainly needed display cases for the laces and places to hang examples of finished dresses, blouses, and other items - not very complicated, but artistic and eclectic touches were integrated to add charm. But the exterior of the shop needed to be really tasteful and attractive, and Constance procured a pink and white awning, with "Katherine Lord's Laces" written in Spencerian gold script on a prominent front glass panel, and on a small hanging sign over the entrance. The door was antique-distressed wood with an antique gold handle, and there was a window display area exhibiting examples of finished lacy dresses that Constance hoped would make every mother drool to make or get something like it.

As Constance was decorating and looking over a couple of lacy dresses she was planning to display, Jeremy asked, "What if a lot of your friends and customers like the finished product, but don't really want to do it themselves? Do you have people lined up who can sew to order, and will you also offer finished products they can buy right off the hanger?"

"That's a good question, Jeremy, and I have thought a lot about it," Constance answered. "The initial concept was to teach customers to do it themselves, make their own little outfits, because that's most of the fun, to do your own creation for your own child, heirlooms that could be handed down from generation to generation. As creators of these works of art, the mothers would take special pride in them and would want the pride and pleasure of doing it themselves. That's what drew me to it, and that's what I wanted to market, the satisfying pleasure of creating a beautiful work of art that one's own children could show off. And yet, I am sure there will be those who just like the 'look' of a finished article and will want their child to be seen in it but aren't willing to make it themselves - either because they don't have time with all the pressure of daily living, or because they lack the confidence that they can ever do the job. If someone looks at it as a job to be done, rather than as a creative activity, like painting a painting, then we have lost that person as far as my original concept is concerned. I see my job as being a kind of missionary to change the way customers look at these clothes. I know they are used to buying clothes off a rack and, at most, altering them to fit the child's age and size, and I know there are some, maybe most, whose mindset cannot be changed, but my hope is that there will be enough who will be open to my way of thinking that I can bring them around and generate enough business and profits to sustain our boutique. After all, we are not trying to build a Fortune 500 company."

"Okay, Connie, whatever you say, but what if you are wrong, and the vast majority of your customers like the finished product but don't want to produce it themselves, just want to buy it? I ask you again, do you have people lined up to make outfits for that category of customers, which might turn out to be what you need in order to make ends meet?" Jeremy asked.

"We do have some backup like that," Constance replied. "We will start out with a modest inventory of finished products that I mainly want to use as examples to inspire customers to want to create their own. I will be willing to sell those items, although not necessarily immediately when the customers want them. I might have to ask them to come back later and get them, to give me time to generate more display items to take their place. And we will have the capability to contract out a request for an outfit of a certain design. However, this is an almost dead or dying art, and there just are not a lot of people available who can turn out these products on demand. That's part of my mission, to build up a healthy interest in beautiful children's clothing.

"One thing you might not be aware of," Constance continued, "is that I am offering kits that contain the right amount of lace, plus patterns that can be made using the lace. Customers can get the rest of the cloth in a lot of places, but the lace is hard to find, and the kits provide the patterns and instructions, which is what they need to get started. And - guess what? I had photos of our children, all dressed up in their laced finery, as the cover of each kit. They are adorable, and I think the kits will sell even if the customers never create the lacy outfits from the kits. That's the best I can do. I am on a mission!"

"Let's keep our fingers crossed that your mission is successful!" Jeremy replied.

CHAPTER FIVE:
The Boutique

It turned out Constance had a beautiful sunny day for her store opening. She had hors d'oeuvres and dainty demitasse cups, and optional cordial glasses for Sherry. And there was sparkling water, too, for Kate and others who might prefer it. Formal invitations had been sent to all the Junior League members and others who Constance assumed might be likely prospects. The store was small, and invitations staggered the times for suggested arrivals, but many disregarded the specified open house hours and simply assumed that a commercial business would always be open and welcoming at all times during normal business hours. The crowds did not disappoint Constance or Kate, who co-hosted the opening of the store. Kate had loose lace samples draped loosely around her neck, and visited with individual patrons, showing off the special laces, and occasionally taking customers over to cabinets holding the main repository of products. Kate would sometimes take the patrons to the back of the store and demonstrate some stitching. Lace was cut to order, kits were sold with the cherubic images of Constance's children, and the displayed lacy outfits were much admired. At the end of the day, lace and lady fingers had seen the store through its first test, but there would be successive days of open houses to follow. One thing that Constance learned was that Jeremy was right: there was proportionately more interest in buying finished designs than in doing the sewing in home parlors, although not to such an extent that Constance was alarmed. She understood that she was doing missionary work and that she needed to make decorative lace converts over time.

The staggered open houses continued, the young mothers kept coming, lace sewing classes regularly convened, and Constance was frequently contacting those with whom she had loosely contracted to sew salable display attire for the young. The euphoria would not last forever. The contract sewers were mainly hobbyists themselves and had no intention of dropping everything to sew garments on Constance's schedule, so there was always a scarcity of salable display items. The customers who had enthusiastically bought lace and kits and had attended some of Kate's sewing classes now seemed either to be occupied with their initial projects or had turned to other more pressing matters. The patronage was attenuating. Constance was sure business would pick up in time. "It's a new business," she told herself. "It takes a while to develop a stable level of patronage. It's a unique boutique, no real competition. And its reputation will grow. I just have to be patient."

She had imagined a delightful environment where she and friends could essentially meet in a sewing club environment and sew for their children and swap ideas for lovely new outfits, and that was indeed a part of it. However, she had not quite factored in the necessity for opening the store at a certain hour, staffing it throughout the day with employees who could knowledgeably answer customer questions, respond to telephone inquiries, handle cash registers, and do gift-wrapping. There was also a sameness to the business, having to be in the same place for almost the entire day - every day. These were all obvious necessities for running a business, but they had gotten lost in the excitement of planning her new boutique. She missed the flexibility to come and go as she pleased, because she felt that either she or Kate Lord needed to be there at all times to meet the expectations of customers. But Constance kept telling herself that the inconveniences of starting a new business were to be expected for a while, but eventually it would all run so smoothly that she would not need to be "on the scene" at all times. Keeping track of inventory and expenses was also one of the practicalities that took some of the shine off the vision. Jeremy did not say much, but Constance imagined he was thinking that she had bitten off too much. Certainly, the boutique contributed little romance to their personal lives, as the new business seemed all consuming.

Constance was not the only principal to begin having reservations about the new venture. Kate and Constance found themselves alone in the back of the shop when it had been open about four months. Kate broached the conversation, "Constance, I have tried to do what I could to be on hand for the opening of the shop, and I hope that has helped. But I have decided this is not for me. I was happy doing my thing from home, working with a small group of dedicated lace enthusiasts, but what had been a pleasure and social activity for me has turned into an all-consuming business, and it just is not something I can go on with. I want to just forfeit my share of the business to you, and leave it all with you,"

Constance was stunned. "Kate, you can't mean that! We're in this thing together. I spent all this money, even named the shop after you. To our customers, you are the face of the shop. Its goodwill rests on your reputation and involvement. You just can't leave me like that. Things will get better over time. Sometimes I feel the way you do, but we've got to keep going. We're on a mission, and we have too much at stake to walk away from it now. My dad loaned the money. He believed in us. We just can't let this happen."

"It was your idea, Constance, not mine. I went along for a while because you were so gung-ho about it, and I couldn't stop you. Frankly, I admired your enthusiasm and determination. But I've given it all I can give. I have another life, and I'm older than you are. I just don't have the commitment to go on, and I have other personal reasons," Kate responded with both determination and fatigue.

"But, Kate, you own forty per cent of the business! Doesn't that mean anything to you? And I gave it to you: you didn't have to invest a penny of your own money, and, as I said, I put your name on the shop. I think we're both a little tired. Let's both go to our homes, get a good night's sleep, and then try to find a way to work this out, tomorrow or the next day. Do you need to take a week off, go somewhere for a break? Why don't you just go ahead now and take a week or so, and then let's talk," Constance offered.

"As I said, you can have my forty per cent interest, Connie. It's not that important to me. I just need to get out. It's all yours. I have made up my mind. I don't think it would help to take time off to think about it, because I am not going to change my mind," Kate announced firmly. Kate got up to leave, looked in her handbag, pulled out some pieces of lace and laid them on the table, and then headed for the door.

"Wait, Kate! Let's try to find a way to make this work. We can get someone like a mediator to help us find a way forward - together," Constance called to her. Kate continued through the door and said nothing.

Constance sat down, running her fingers through her sandy hair, noticing that her temples were damp with worry sweat. She thought, "Kate doesn't know how to let me down gently, does she? She used a sledgehammer, and I was totally unprepared. I still can't believe this has happened. There's got to be a way out, a way to salvage this project." She became faintly aware that one of her salespersons was talking with a customer in the front of the shop. She went up front and joined in the conversation. "What a neat shop you have!" said the customer.

"It was a dream of mine," Constance replied, "and I've come to realize that dreams have their own reality, have to be nurtured and encouraged. Sometimes I wonder about the difference between a dream and a nightmare!" The customer chuckled, but, to Constance, it was not small talk.

CHAPTER SIX:
Picking Up the Pieces

Constance had gone to see her father, the Professor. "Dad, I am so sorry to bother you. You have been so generous and understanding, always. I tried to talk with Jeremy, but he has no sympathy or empathy at all - NONE! He says he always had his doubts about the business, but I was determined to go ahead with it. Now it's my problem, and I just have to deal with it myself, leave him out of it. He doesn't even want me to bring up the subject, much less offer me advice. He says it has affected our home life and marital relations, and maybe it has, and I'm sorry, but I need help and advice. So, I've come to you, with embarrassment for my predicament, but knowing you always have good advice, and I need it!"

"Okay. I'm here, and I'm listening. Tell me all about it," said Professor Selsby. "You say Kate has threatened to walk out on you, or maybe she has done that. That leaves you alone on the front lines. But I think it might be helpful for your own sake, just in thinking through the problem, if you would start from the beginning."

"Well, it came out of the blue, Daddy. The shop has not been an entirely smooth ride, has had its share of bumps along the way, and there have been times I got tired of it, too, but I knew - or should have known - to expect that. You have to get the kinks out of every new business, and I kept telling myself that this was just par for the course, what you have to expect. I worked hard to learn the business, but I was blind, or naïve, about the most important part.

Kate was my partner, and now I realize that I didn't know Kate. You think you know a person, but you really never know anyone when you get to the core of their character, and what goes on inside. Kate seemed excited at first, pitched in and helped with the open houses and general startup. At times she seemed to be slacking off a bit, but I am sure I did, too - it's natural. But most new entrepreneurs stick with it until things are better, or in the worst of cases, if things go sour, until you reach the end of the road. But then Kate dropped her ton of bricks on me, when we were just getting started, four months into the program," Constance began.

"Kate is a somewhat older person, isn't she?" Professor Selsby asked.

"Well, yes, she is, probably in her mid-to-late fifties, but she has always seemed to have vitality. You would not think retirement would be on her mind, and I have never heard her allude to any particular medical problems. What I can't understand is that she never would identify any specific kind of problem or issue that pushed her to abandon ship. If she would just say, 'I have a problem with this,' or 'so-and-so bothers me,' then we could address those specifics, and maybe we could work something out, but she only tells me she's had enough, that she has decided the shop is not for her, and she is walking out, firm decision made. I feel so bad because you funded the business, and you had confidence in me, and I've let you down," Constance sobbed in her bewilderment and regret.

"The past is passed, Constance. We have to focus on the present and the future. How's your legal documentation of the deal? Sometimes, if you have to get lawyers involved, they can get through to the parties when nothing else can - you know, nobody likes going to Court, except maybe the lawyers!" her dad probed.

"That is what I am really sorry about. Dad. You told me to get a lawyer involved in setting everything up, but Kate and I were so congenial, and the deal seemed simple, we just wrote it out on one or two sheets of paper, in my handwriting. The business is not even incorporated; it is just a partnership between Kate and me. There are no provisions for dealing with a breakup of the business," Constance confessed.

"I see," said Professor Selsby, trying not to show his dismay. "Then you have never consulted Ted Born, the lawyer?"

"No, but I guess that's the next thing I need to do," Constance surmised.

"I think that's right. Otherwise, you won't know what your options are. I would go and see him as soon as you can get an appointment. And, Constance, I'm still here, with two good ears for listening, and I'm on your side. Whatever mistakes or miscalculations have been made, you don't deserve what has happened to you. I will still be here, whenever we need to talk. I'm proud of the initiative you have taken," the Professor said comfortingly and with genuine affection.

Constance was able to get an appointment with Ted Born within a couple of days and went to visit him. Born was younger than Constance had expected, roughly her own age, probably mid-to-late thirties. He listened intently and sympathetically to his client's dilemma and looked at her paperwork, and said, "Your paperwork is not what I would have hoped, Constance, but that does not mean you don't have rights. One of the main problems is that your paperwork doesn't cover contingencies, what your remedies would be in case of a melt-down in your relationship with Kate. There is also vagueness as to just what Kate's responsibilities were, how much work exactly she was expected to do, and for how long. Your contract rights are not what we would prefer. But there is a doctrine in the law called 'promissory estoppel' which mean that, once someone makes a promise to you - even an oral promise - and you change your position in reliance on that promise, the promiser cannot renege on the promise, and the law will recognize and enforce the promise, provided it is not a promise by a singer to give a concert or something like that, where the courts are not suited to judge the performance.

"Now, although your paperwork doesn't state precisely how long Kate was to perform her duties, I think the law would presume she would need to perform them for a reasonable period of time based on the nature of the relationship, and certainly she jumped overboard long before it was reasonable to expect her to do so, that is, before the enterprise had a fair opportunity to prove itself. There is one other issue: If you were abusive, so as to make the relationship intolerable to continue, Kate might be able to argue that she was entitled to get free from an intolerable relationship. Have you had any disagreement or conflicts that Kate could point to as a justification for her abrupt departure?"

"None whatsoever," Constance replied. "That's what made it such a shock. As far as I could tell, we had always had an excellent relationship, never a cross word between us. We were working hard, of course, right alongside each other, but we would both joke and smile about it and do our jobs. Even though one might expect some sources of friction in a startup relationship, miraculously, we had none, and certainly not any that could be described as a conflict or even a significant difference of opinion."

"Glad to hear that, but, of course, Kate might have a different recollection or impression, real or imagined. Does Kate have a lawyer, as far as you know?" Born asked.

"I have no idea, never heard her mention one," Constance responded.

"Have you been in touch with Kate at all since the day she walked out on you?" Ted asked.

"No, I haven't heard from her, and I wanted to get some advice before initiating a contact," Constance answered.

"Then I would suggest you write her a very nice and conciliatory letter suggesting a mutually happy resolution and a willingness to negotiate. I would hope such a letter might actually accomplish a reconciliation. But, if it does not, the jury will understand that you tried to work things out, that you tried to be a peacemaker and do the right thing, and the jury will look more favorably on your case if she ignores your entreaty or chooses to spit in your face. If that effort does not bear fruit, I would suggest drafting a complaint to be filed in Court and sending it to her with the request that she share it with her lawyer and ask her lawyer to contact me. Kate might listen to the advice of her own lawyer, even if she avoids communicating with you or me. If she gets a lawyer so that I can deal directly with him or her, we might make some progress as she listens to the advice of her own lawyer. The hope is that we can avoid going to Court by taking these initial steps, but of course a lawsuit might end up being inevitable."

Constance wrote the suggested letter to Kate, and Ted Born reviewed and edited it, written with the hope it could lead to reconciliation but, in any case, it would show the Judge and jury that Constance was trying for reconciliation. The letter was mailed, and Constance nervously checked her incoming mail and her telephone messages for a possible response. There was nothing. Kate was obviously ignoring the letter, and thereby rejecting any notion of reconciliation or resolution. Ted then drafted a comprehensive complaint, ready to be filed in Court, and mailed it to Kate, requesting that she share the letter and draft complaint with her lawyer. In a few days, Ted got a telephone call from attorney Zack Odom. "Hi, Ted. Kate Lord shared your letter with me and asked me to call you," Zack began. Ted and Zack knew each other, though not really well, and Ted thought Zack was an able and reliable attorney.

"Zack, I appreciate your calling, and I am relieved that you are Kate's lawyer because I admire your good judgment, and that should make it easier to work things out. These are both nice ladies, as far as I can tell, and it's a shame we are at this crossroad. What's your take on the situation, and what do you see as the crux of the problem?" Ted inquired.

"Ted, you should first understand that I am not Kate's regular lawyer; in fact, I don't think she has a regular lawyer. Someone just suggested she contact me. I don't have a contract with her to serve as her lawyer, but I told her I would give you a call, for what it's worth. So, I don't have any authority to 'make a deal.' I am just a volunteer, trying to be helpful if I can," Zack explained.

"Well, Zack, maybe you can help with a fundamental question we have: What's the crux of the problem? All we know is that Kate said she didn't want to be involved with the shop anymore and walked away. We can't solve any problems unless we know what they are," Ted said, trying to get a clue.

"I don't know what to say, Ted. She just says she doesn't want to do it anymore. It was an abrupt change in her lifestyle, and it's not for her. She just wants 'out.' Doesn't sound like there is any particular issue that can be addressed and 'solved,'" Zack said.

"Surely there must be something there that could help, like more flexible working hours, fewer classes and appearances, maybe more money - though that would be a tough one for a fledgling little startup that's been losing money from Day One. Maybe a few weeks away from the store, just to think about it. There ought to be a way. Two nice people shouldn't be at loggerheads like this. Let's try to help them," Ted urged.

"I don't know, Ted. Kate seems to have made her mind up. I don't think there is going to be anything we can say or do that will change her. She really just wanted me to deliver a message to you and Constance that she is really and truly finished with the project, and please leave her alone. She doesn't seem to care anything about her forty per cent interest," Zack pronounced with a note of finality.

"But, Zack, surely, she is rational, and surely she understands how this abrupt departure at a critical time leaves Constance in the lurch. Surely, we can work something out," Ted pleaded.

"I will pass along what you have said, Ted, but I am just a lawyer with a very limited portfolio. I have my marching orders, and I have said all I can say at this point. Got to move on," Zack said.

"Okay, but let's give ourselves a week or so to see if there is any softening of Kate's position. We won't do anything until we've given it that chance. If we don't hear back, then we will know there is no hope for a voluntary solution. Thanks for calling," Ted said as he hung up the phone. "How to figure that?" Ted asked himself as he frowned. "The situation cries out for compromise, and there ought to be a way to make a compromise deal, but Kate's intransigence just makes no sense to me." He reported the conversation to Constance, and they prepared to allow Kate a week before taking legal action, but neither of them was optimistic.

CHAPTER SEVEN:
The Fat in the Fire

The week following Ted's phone call with Zack Odom had passed, and there was total silence from Zack and Kate. Constance called Ted, "Well, Ted, we've given them a week, and nothing's happened. What do we do now?"

"Constance, you really don't have any choice but to file a lawsuit, which will cost money, and I have no idea whether Kate has assets that we could look to for collection of any verdict we might get. First, tell me how the business is going," Ted replied.

"As for the business, we are stumbling along. Customers are asking for Kate and want to sign up for Kate's classes. I've recruited a person who worked with Kate, like I once did, and who is really very good, and she is teaching some classes. I'm not sure she will want to do that on a long-term basis, but it is helping for right now. Some of our dressmakers want to work only through Kate, and I'm trying to get them to work directly with me. I think some will come over, and some probably will not. The lace suppliers have not been a problem thus far, and that's been good. There has been a falloff in business overall, and I suspect it is going to get worse when customers find out Kate is no longer on the team. I obviously am trying to keep the doors open, because I am stuck with it and don't know what else to do. As for Kate and whether any judgment against her would be collectible, I have heard her say that she inherited a farm out in the country, I think a pretty good-sized farm, not too far from town, and it probably has some value. Obviously, I have no idea about her bank account or whether she owns any stocks. Somehow, she gets by financially and doesn't seem to need the income the new business could produce. I don't think she could be getting Social Security quite yet. She's unmarried, divorced, I gather. If she has any children, I don't think they live around here," Constance answered.

"Constance, nothing is sure in litigation, you know," Ted observed. "Also, my law firm doesn't work on a contingent-fee basis. You understand, that's where a lawyer agrees to get paid only if he or she wins the case and then gets a percentage of the recovery. We get paid by the amount of time we put in, win or lose. You could lose, as your paperwork is not in great shape, and even if you win, it might not be enough to compensate you fairly. And, of course, we can't be sure any judgment would be collectible. Are you able and willing to pay us a retainer and pay our monthly bills as we go forward, knowing that you might not come out ahead in the end?"

"My dad recommended you to me, Ted. I think he would stand behind me on this, but I need to check with him about it. As you said, I don't think I have any choice but to file suit. I just can't accept Kate's decision to leave me in the lurch like this, and she hasn't even apologized for doing it. Let's get ready to file suit, and I will confirm the financial arrangements," Constance said, trying to assure herself that Professor Selsby would indeed back up the financial aspects.

`Constance later called back and said she had the financial backing for the lawsuit, and asked Ted to proceed with it. "But, Ted," she commented, "You have this complaint written as a demand for money. Couldn't you ask the Court to order her to come back and perform her duties? That's what I was counting on when I decided to open the store. I would much prefer her to come back than to get money. Can't we take that approach?"

"I wish we could, Constance, but I don't think so. You can ask for an injunction to prevent someone from doing an active wrong to you, but courts are very reluctant to order an individual to perform personal services. For one thing, your paperwork is vague as to exactly what she was to do. More importantly, courts cannot very satisfactorily stand over a person and supervise their performance and can't really distinguish between superior work and subnormal work. A classic case is the opera star situation. What if the Court were to order an opera star to perform and the opera star sings off-key? It could be accidental, but it could be intentional, and courts are not in a good position to police that kind of thing. I think we have to frame this complaint in terms of asking for a money judgment. Still, the threat of Kate's losing and having to pay you a lot of money might have a sobering effect, and it's possible Kate will decide it's better to settle with you - and, preferably on the basis of coming back and carrying out her commitments - than to go through a lawsuit and suffer its possible monetary consequences. Litigation sometimes has a way of providing a reality check, a softening up of hardnosed positions. But, of course, you can't count on that," Ted advised.

"Maybe there's hope, then. If we win and get some money, that will help, but it won't solve my problems. I will still have a shop on my hands that I have to deal with somehow. I opened it under the assumption Kate would be partnering with me, and that major assumption seems to have been dashed. I can see the possibility, maybe the probability, of having to close the shop eventually, whether or not we win the lawsuit. Jeremy is very unsympathetic. He has an 'I-told-you-so' attitude. He's of no help. He says it's none of his doing, it's my problem, and I just have to deal with it. I have this feeling of abandonment, first by Kate, and now by my own husband. I'm glad you're on my side, Ted. How long is it going to be before we have a trial? What's our timeframe?" Constance asked.

"I know what you are thinking: How long do I have to keep this ship afloat, or is it even possible to keep it afloat until we have a trial? I wish I knew the answer. It depends on the Judge we draw, and the status of the docket, and how much resistance we get from Kate and her lawyer. The case is not terribly complicated. There are not many witnesses - mainly you and Kate - and not many documents. We will have to develop expert witness testimony on the calculation of your damages. In other words, it should not take a lot of trial preparation, and it should only require a day or two to try the case. I will do what I can to move it along, but it is not something we can control. I will have a better feel for it after the case is filed and we see who our Judge is and who Kate's lawyer is. She might or might not use Zack Odom as her trial lawyer, as he told me he was only hired as a one-shot deal, to deliver a message to me. Things will begin to clear up, but it could conceivably take a year or two," Ted speculated.

"A year or two!! My God! I'm not sure I can last for a year or two with this albatross around my neck! Ted, please do what you can to speed it up, PLLEEASE!" Constance implored.

The complaint was filed, and Ted was pleased that his case was assigned to Judge Higgins, whom Ted had always found was reasonable to work with, not autocratic at all. He also got a telephone call from Zack Odom, advising Ted that he would be representing Kate in the litigation. Zack made an encouraging comment in his phone call. "Ted, quite frankly, my client is very budget conscious and feels she wants to defend herself but does not want a long and drawn-out trial. This is a pretty simple case, and I wonder if we can work together to get an early trial. It will help everyone to get it behind us. Just let me warn you, though - and I guess you probably already know this - there's not a pot of gold at the end of this rainbow. My client lives a simple and modest life. I get the feeling she will never agree to come back, but at least we can get it behind us without it taking forever."

Ted tried to appear casual and not reveal his being overjoyed by the hope of a prompt trial. "Zack," he said, "I am going to try to be flexible and cooperative in working together with you in our clients' interests. A lot depends on the Judge's docket, of course, but I would not be opposed to trying to get a special setting that could expedite things. I am sure you and I both have busy schedules with other cases, and we will have to see what we can work out. But I'm willing to explore an early special setting. We of course will want to take your client's deposition in advance of trial, and you will probably want to take Constance's. Let's check with our clients and then check with Judge Higgins to see what we can do."

"Manna from heaven!" Ted said to himself as he concluded the phone call. He then called Constance, who was working at her shop. "Connie, a great thing has just happened. I got a call from Zack Odom who confirmed to me that he would be representing Kate, but he indicated he's working under a budget and needs to move the case along as fast as we can. I nearly fell out of my chair when he said that, but I tried to be nonchalant, told him I was willing to try to cooperate with him but that it would depend on a lot of things. Between you and me, I think there is a good chance Judge Higgins will agree to try to work us in on a special setting that will expedite the trial greatly, if we assure him both sides are ready to go. It means we really have to be ready, having taken Kate's deposition and having found an expert witness to quantify our claim of damages. I can't say this solves everything, but it opens up a window of opportunity to getting a faster resolution, rather than an extended one."

"Music to my ears, Ted, although I would rather have had a more conciliatory message from Kate. Do what you can. You can count on my full cooperation," Constance said.

"I will warn you of something in advance, though. We need for this to be a jury trial. We've demanded trial by jury, but it could be waived. However, I think it would be a mistake to waive a jury trial in order to speed things up, because Judge Higgins - from my past experience - is pretty conservative in awarding damages. So, even if it takes a little longer, we need to have a jury trial. And that will call for special sacrifice on your part, Constance," Ted said.

"Like what, Ted?" Constance asked.

"Like, I am going to ask you to put away those flashy rings on your fingers and the designer necklaces and dresses. You are going to have to look the part of a betrayed shop owner trying to get by, and not a wealthy heiress. And you will need to tone down the perfume. Some jurors are allergic to perfume, and others will take it as a badge of upper-class privilege. Simplicity, and plainness, will be your watchwords. Don't get me wrong. You have style, classy style, and I like that, and your circle of friends like that, but you will need to come across to the jury more like I imagine Kate to be, plain and simple - but, in your case, betrayed! We are trying to communicate with the jury and get them to focus on what happened to you, and not be distracted by jewelry and perfume. Trials are all about communicating the right message to the jury, without any distractions. You will be making a stage presentation, in a sense. Imagine what you want the jury to get out of it. But of course, we will have plenty of time to go over all of this as we get closer to trial time," Ted explained.

CHAPTER EIGHT:
Domestic Tranquility

It was a Sunday morning, when Jeremy was not "on call" to deal with medical inquiries or emergencies from his pediatric patients, and Constance had a brief break from her shop. The children, four-year old Angela and three-year old Remy, had finished their breakfasts and were playing in the den where all sorts of toys had been strewn about the floor. Constance and Jeremy were having sweet rolls and coffee at the breakfast room table from which there was an angled view of the den. Constance spoke first, "Jeremy, we haven't seen much of each other lately, and I have a guilty feeling about it. I've been so focused on the shop, and so worried about Kate's walkout on me, I really haven't been myself, and I feel a sort of distance between us. I know it's my fault, and I don't like it, so I want to apologize."

"Connie, I know. I know it's not like it used to be, and I think we both thought and hoped your preoccupation with the shop would be a temporary thing, but now it's looking more and more like it is endless, and, besides that, you're about to have litigation with Kate. It was your project, and I didn't want to hold you back, but neither of us could have guessed it would turn out this way. We've hired this nanny to help with the children on weekdays, and that helps. But she's also another person - a stranger - hanging around in the house, impinging on our privacy, even though she is trying to be an active tutor as well as a caregiver. It allows you to spend a lot of time at the shop, but there is a privacy price we are also paying, to say nothing of her salary," Jeremy reflected.

Constance began to sob, "Just bear with me, show me you care, tell me you still love me. I know we will find a way to make it all work out. We just need some more time, and some good luck."

"How's business at the shop? Still holding up?" Jeremy asked.

"Actually, it seems to have tapered off some - which was to be expected. The early bloom is gone, but it is probably a seasonal thing - I hope. Still, it doesn't help that Kate is not on hand to give advice - advice to me and to customers - and teach classes. I'm just taking it one day at a time and trying to keep a smiley face toward my friends and customers, telling them how thrilled I am to have this nice boutique!" Constance said ruefully.

"How can you keep your smiley face on when they all sooner or later find out you are in a lawsuit with Kate, who is the namesake of the shop?" Jeremy asked.

"I don't know, Jeremy. I just don't know! I have been pondering that question over and over. I don't have any choice but to sue her. She was wrong to walk out on me for no good reason. And yet - you are right - it's not going to be good for business. I guess I will just have to explain my side to the customers, and maybe they, or at least some of them, might be sympathetic. But I can't just keep living in limbo. I've got this shop, but the game has changed, and running the shop indefinitely on my own is not good for me, or for our family relationships. I'm caught, Jeremy, I'm cornered, and the future is all screwed up. I don't know where to go. For now, I have to try to trust Ted Born, who is a take-charge kind of guy. He's decisive, doesn't try to avoid hard decisions. He agrees we have to sue Kate. Then the question is: win or lose the lawsuit, what do I do next? Just trudge down to the shop, day after day - for how long? And what is the end game? I don't know the answers, but I'm looking for them. I still think it was a good idea, but it went bad."

Constance shook her head in despair over her situation, and her seemingly lost dream. Just then, Angela and Remy bounded out of the den, apparently tired of their toys and playtime, wanting to see what was going on with Mama and Daddy.

Constance leaned over and put an arm around Angela and squeezed. Then she patted Remy on the head. Neither of them was dressed in their lacy finery, and Constance remarked, "I'm glad I have the pictures of you two in your fancy outfits, and I'm glad they're on the front of the kits I'm selling at the shop. It's the one thing that makes Mama happy when I am at the shop, just to look at pictures of my precious children. I love you so much!"

"Mama, can we go down to your shop and stay with you? That would be fun, and maybe we could help," Angela asked.

"Oh, I would love to have you at the shop, at least for a little while, someday. I'll try to figure out a time when it's not so busy. You know, it's a small shop, and we don't have any toys there. I think you might get bored. And what would you do with your nanny? She would miss you. But maybe we can do it someday," Constance answered.

"But, Mama, Nanny said you have lollipops at the store. You could give me a lollipop," Remy said.

"Remy, Mama will bring you TWO lollipops from the shop the next time I go! And two for Angela! Would you like, lime or cherry flavored lollipops?" their mother asked. They each opted for one of each kind.

"Mama, guess what I did? I just taught Remy the 'eensy, weensy spider' rhyme," Angela announced.

Constance and Jeremy both smiled. "Remy, tell us about the eensy, weensy spider. Can you do that?" Remy took both hand and recited the rhyme, illustrating with his hands how the "eensy, weensy spider" climbed up the waterspout, and how the rain came and washed the spider out, and then the sun came and dried up all the rain, and the "eensy, weensy spider" went up the spout again. The family clapped for Remy when he finished, and Remy joined in the clapping.

Connie looked at Jeremy and said, "You know, our home should have more of that. It's called pride of achievement, and the world needs a lot more of it, too. Yes, domestic tranquility! Nothing in the world should be able to crowd out the 'eensy, weensy spider' moments of sheer joy and happiness." Jeremy agreed the world could definitely benefit if only there were more "eensy, weensy spider" moments of innocence and joy, with troubles at bay in the far distance.

CHAPTER NINE:
The Deposition

Zack Odom filed a "Motion to Dismiss" the complaint. He had no realistic expectation that the Court would grant the motion, but it was a standard practice, tolerated by some Judges, to gain a short reprieve from filing a formal answer. The expectation was that the Judge would overrule the motion and then allow the defendant a certain amount of time to file an answer, sometimes providing a longer period than the standard time allowed for a response under the procedural rules. It also served as an occasion for the opposing counsel to discuss their case and get a feel for what to expect from the other side, and from the Court. Sometimes the Judge would get involved in communicating with the lawyers in a way that offered some clues - and perhaps some informal advice to the parties - as to the Judge's perception of the case. Input from the Judge was often minimal, depending on how crowded the motion docket was on the appointed day, and whether the case was a jury trial or a non-jury bench trial. Judges were generally more reticent to get involved at an early stage in a non-jury case for fear of tainting their impartiality when they would ultimately be the triers of the facts, unlike the more limited role they play when there is a jury.

So it was that Ted Born and Zack Odom appeared in Judge Higgins' courtroom to argue Zack's motion. The motion docket was not very crowded that day, and, because the lawsuit was the most recent on the docket, the argument was heard at the very end of proceedings, when the courtroom was clearing from the departure of those who had already made their arguments. It did not appear there would be any real argument by either Zack or Ted. The Judge picked up Zack's motion and Ted's complaint and looked at Zack. Seeing the motion for what it was, he peered over his spectacles, and said, "Zack, what do you need, another twenty days to file your answer?"

Zack smiled and said, "That would be appreciated, Your Honor."

"All right, you've got your twenty days. Looking at the complaint and attached 'agreement,' I just wonder, will you be contesting that the alleged promises were made by Katherine Lord?" Judge Higgins asked.

"Well, Judge, we might be making some contentions about the so-called 'agreement,' but we have other defenses that we will argue excused performance," Zack answered.

"Looks like this could be a fairly simple case," the Judge observed. "Shouldn't take but a day or so to try. Have you attempted to settle it?"

Zack looked at Ted and then answered. "Your Honor, we have had some brief conversations about it, but I'm not sure you could call them settlement discussions. I'm not sure our clients are of a mind to do that. This could be one of those cases you just have to go all the way to trial, because of the personalities, even if it looks like it ought to be settled."

"Zack, I'm sure you know that there are worse things that can happen than to settle, and Ted has demanded a jury trial. I just suggest that it is always a good idea to make a good faith settlement effort, because, if the case is ever going to be settled, before you get too invested in it, it is better to settle now than later. I'm going back into my chambers, but I think it would be worth your taking a few minutes to just stay here in the courtroom and see if you can work out something, or at least get started on working it out. Okay, for the time being, I have entered my order denying the motion to dismiss and allowing the defendant twenty additional days to answer."

The Judge left the courtroom, and Ted and Zack looked at each other. Ted said, "Zack, I am perfectly willing to see if we can work it out. My client has no animosity toward your client, and in fact Constance admires and thinks the world of your client. There's lots of goodwill from our side, and I hope from your side as well. Why can't they just put things back together again and take up where they left off? We could put the lawsuit and any ill feelings behind us and work together as friends in a common cause. Make sense?"

"It might make sense, Ted, but I doubt it's going to happen. I think there are other issues involved," Zack responded.

"Like what?" asked Ted.

"I really don't know, Ted. Kate keeps her own counsel, doesn't seem to want to talk about it. She just says she's not going to work on the boutique project anymore, and she seems to be saying to me that her decision is final," Zack answered, with a slight shake of the head.

"Obviously, we will want to take Kate's deposition. Can we do that pretty soon, like within thirty days or so?" Ted inquired.

"I don't see why not," Zack offered. "I think we should both move this case along as fast as we can. My client just cannot afford the legal expenses of drawn-out litigation. I'll try to get a few open dates from her and get back to you."

The two lawyers parted company, and Ted went back to his office and telephoned Constance. "Connie, I have just come back from the courthouse. The Judge denied the motion to dismiss, as expected, and gave Kate's lawyer Zack twenty days to answer. The interesting thing is that I got the feeling the Judge felt Kate had a questionable position and urged the two lawyers to discuss settlement. And that's what we did, right there in the Judge's courtroom after he left the room and returned to his chambers. But, if I can trust what Zack is saying, he doesn't have a clue what the core problem is for Kate. He says she keeps it to herself but is firm on not being willing to restore the relationship with the boutique. I assured him you had no ill will toward Kate and urged him to see if he could find a way to work things out. But I have to say, I'm not optimistic. Sometimes, though, you have to soften people up a little bit, let them learn the lesson that litigation is not fun - and can be expensive. Sometimes, people begin to reconsider things they once rejected out of hand, *after* they have gotten a taste of litigation. I want you to be there, looking across the table at her as she answers my questions."

"Whatever you say, Ted. I just wish I knew what caused her sudden withdrawal, after the months of planning and opening the shop, and having all the open houses. I've wondered if money was the issue, that she didn't feel like she was being compensated properly. But we could talk through money issues. It seems that there is something else behind the walkout. It's a mystery. It can't be a problem with the clientele, because Kate has been working with most of our really good customers for a long time. Maybe we can find out and come up with a fix for it," Constance said wistfully.

The day of the deposition came, and the parties all assembled in a conference room at Ted's office. Neither Constance and Kate showed any hostility toward each other, and, in fact, they chatted pleasantly but briefly before the deposition began. The Court reporter was present to take down the questions and answers in the deposition. Ted began by asking Kate some questions which were not contentious, her background, how she got into lace, and how it came about that she met Constance and how they decided to start the Katherine Lord Lace shop.

Ted: "How did you decide how to finance the shop?"

Kate: "Connie said she would finance it and suggested that we would each have a financial interest in the shop. She would have 60%, and I would have 40%."

Ted: "Did you negotiate with Constance over those suggested figures?"

Kate: "No, I accepted them."

Ted: "Did you consider at the time that a 60/40 split, where Connie would have the majority ownership, was fair and reasonable?"

Kate: "I had no problem with that split. It seemed fair to me since she was putting in all the money."

Ted: "Has anything happened since that time to change your mind as to whether that was a fair deal?"

Kate: "No. It still seems fair to me."

Ted: "You were also to be compensated for your time at the store and for teaching classes?"

Kate: "Yes. I had no problem with that."

Ted: "Have you been paid the agreed upon amounts for your services at the shop?"

Kate: "Yes."

Ted: "Has anything occurred up to the present time to cause you to think that the financial arrangements for your services at the shop were unfair or unreasonable?"

Kate: "No."

Ted: "Did you understand at the beginning that the shop was a risk venture and might not be profitable, or that it might take a long time before it became profitable?"

Kate: "Oh, yes. I knew it might take a while for the shop to make money. The financial aspects were never an issue with me."

Ted: "Did anyone ever mistreat or insult you or do anything wrong to you during the time you were working at the Shop?"

Kate: "No, not that I can think of at this time."

Ted: "Was Constance or any of the shop employees ever rude to you or did anything unfair to you?"

Kate: "No, they have always been very kind."

Ted: "Then what was your reason for cutting off your relationship with Constance and the shop?"

Kate: "I would rather not say."

Ted: "You understand, Mrs. Lord, that the purpose of this deposition is for Constance to get answers to questions relevant, or possibly relevant, to the complaint that has been filed. Have you read the complaint?"

Kate: "Yes, I have."

Ted: "Then you should understand that your leaving the shop and refusing to come back is what the whole lawsuit is about. So, I have to insist that you answer my question."

Kate: "I don't want anybody to get hurt. I did what I thought I had to do."

Ted: "What kind of hurt were you trying to avoid?"

Kate: "Harm to Constance."

Ted: "What kind of harm?"

Kate: "I'm not sure. I could just foresee it, something really bad."

Ted looked at Constance, who was frowning, trying to make sense of Kate's testimony. Ted continued: "Mrs. Lord, please tell us everything you know, or felt, that led you to break your relationship with Constance and the shop."

Kate: "I didn't want to have to go into this, and I know you will think I'm some sort of weirdo kook, but my lawyer has given me the signal that I have to answer, so I guess I have no choice. Do you know what a 'seer' is? I am a seer, have been ever since I was a child. At times, I have dreams or see visions. They're usually clear to me, and I have the ability to look into the future, and what I see almost always comes true."

Ted: "Go on, continue."

Kate: "I had a dream, and Helicon Heights was at the center of it. It was a dark night with a bright moon, and for some reason I found myself outside the house and went to the door, opened it, and stepped inside. It was all quiet at first. Suddenly, I felt I was able to see into the master bedroom, and there were two dark, shadowy figures standing over the bed, and I could tell Constance was in that bed, but she wasn't moving. The figures laughed. I could see something terrible had happened to Constance. I was frightened and left the house."

Ted: "Then what happened?"

Kate: "I woke up in a cold sweat and couldn't go back to sleep. The next morning, I decided I had to get away from Constance and the shop, so I told Constance I was withdrawing. I really couldn't tell her why I did that, because she would have thought I was stark crazy, and it might have worried her. She might have thought the dream represented some Freudian ill-will I bore toward her, but that wasn't true. I was torn between seeming to be disloyal, on the one hand, and a basket case, on the other hand. What could I do? I just kept my reasons to myself."

Ted: "Was there anything else, other than the dream you just described, that caused you to quit your association with Ms. Stanfield and stop participating in the Katherine Lord Lace shop?"

Kate: "No, it was the dream. When I had that revelation of what was going to happen, I knew I could not continue."

Ted: "Mrs. Lord, did you give any consideration to how it would affect Constance and your joint project by withdrawing from her and the shop?"

Kate: "I doubted anything I could do would help her. I considered her fate had been sealed, and there was nothing I could do to help her - or harm her. I just knew I could not let myself be a part of whatever forces were out there, grinding on toward her future demise. I couldn't do that. I had to get out."

Ted: "You say you didn't want to harm her, but didn't you see that it would greatly harm Constance financially to leave her in the lurch with the shop, after she had depended on your involvement when she opened the shop?"

Kate: "I looked at it this way. I was there during the opening weeks of the shop when she needed me most. The shop is either going to succeed or fail on its own merits. I'm giving up my interest in the shop. I'm not indispensable. She can get others. For the sake of my own mental health, I felt I had to get out, and I think that was fair."

Ted: "You say you are a seer. What other experiences have you had, where you believed you had seen the future and it came true, and have your visions of the future always been about bad things happening?"

Kate: "So far, the dreams or visions have mostly been about bad happenings. Some of them have already happened. Others are still in the future, to happen. But they will all happen in due time. Three of them have happened just as I visualized them - my younger brother in an automobile accident, a loss of my uncle in foreign combat and my father losing a fortune in business. Actually, I have had a lot of minor incidents. My family and a few close friends all know I am a seer. My doctor says I'm sane. I don't want to talk about the other incidents. They are very personal. It's a curse I have, and a terrible burden. I wish I was like other people and didn't have this quirk about me. But I go on, as best I can."

Ted: "Can you describe in any detail at all the shadowy figures you saw hovering around Constance's bed? For example, were they men? Were they large or small, anything at all that you can remember?'

Kate: "One was a man, and he seemed to be wearing an overcoat, but his face was blurred. The other one could have been a woman. It seems that, when they laughed, one of them seemed to have a higher-pitched laugh. But the faces were all blurred, and my general impression is just that they were dark figures. It all has begun to fade in my memory with time. I didn't write anything down at the time, as I thought my involvement was all over."

Ted: "And you liked and had a good relationship with Constance, but you didn't share any of this with her at the time?"

Kate: "She would have either laughed it off, or she would have dismissed me as a lunatic, the bright moon shining in my dream correlating with my lunacy. Nobody would have given any credence to this; better to keep it to myself, and just hope that somehow my seer capability was offtrack this time. It's my fervent hope that I am all wrong. I kept my own counsel and wanted to go on with my life and hoped Constance could also, but without me."

After the deposition, Kate smiled at Constance and gave a slight wave as she and her attorney left Ted's conference room, followed by the Court reporter. Constance had looked stunned and bewildered, but she nodded weakly toward Kate. Ted and Constance looked at each other, speechless at first with blank, wondering expressions on their faces. Ted was the first to speak, "What do you make of that, Connie? Did you see that coming?"

"Ted, it is all so weird, so crazy, but I'm shaken. I've never had anyone before who predicted my death - right to my face. I know it wasn't a threat from Kate herself. I assume she has a genuine concern that I am a marked woman. It's cuckoo, of course. I'm just a little shop owner trying to keep the shop running. I don't know where any threat could come from. Of course, we are living in a nice home that I guess some would call a mansion, and some burglar might think there are storerooms of treasure there for the taking, if they ever got in. But we do have a good security system. I don't think I have any enemies. All my friends are nice people. I just am shell-shocked, emotionally, but can't logically make any sense of it," Constance struggled to respond.

"Connie, I think this is rubbish. Obviously, you should be careful, but I would not want you to let it wreck your life, looking around every corner, wondering if there's an assassin hiding there. I don't know much about psychics - not something they dealt with in law school - but I intend to read up on the subject. Meanwhile, my present inclination is to play Kate - gently - as a mental case, a few screws loose somewhere, and you have been victimized by her irrational conduct. Obviously, she will never come back and participate at the shop. And I don't think you would want her, now that you know this side of her. Still, winning the lawsuit is not a sure thing. The jury could see you as a rich speculator eager to exploit Kate's name and relationship, and they could feel sorry for Kate, who is somewhat sympathetic, and let her off Scot-free. But I would hope we could counter all that and successfully portray *you* as an innocent victim, damaged by an insane and groundless imagined scenario. Let's both be thinking about it."

"Yes. I guess I really, R-E-A-L-L-Y, didn't know Kate. I have just been listening in that deposition to something that could have come from the Planet Mars - totally alien to the Kate I thought I knew," Constance voiced ruefully, shaking her head.

CHAPTER TEN:
Dr. Bezic

Kate Lord's deposition introduced an unexpected issue into Constance Stanfield's case. Ted at times felt inclined to laugh about it, but then, he acknowledged to himself that Kate seemed deadly serious. The "deadly" part worried Ted. Perhaps Kate herself was harboring violent inner feelings toward Constance, but that seemed out of character for Kate. In any event, it was an issue which would come out at trial, and it had to be dealt with, viewed from the perspective of jurors. As a lawyer, he could not just ridicule Kate; some jurors might be offended by that. Some jurors might genuinely believe in seers and visions and could be very sympathetic toward Kate. Ted decided he should consult a psychologist. After making some inquiries, he came across the bio sketch for Dr. Martin Bezic, a practicing psychologist and part-time professor at the University, with degrees from Yale College and Duke graduate school. He made an appointment to see Dr. Bezic and sent him a copy of Kate Lord's deposition with the request that Dr. Bezic read it in advance of the appointment.

At the appointment, Ted said, "Dr. Bezic, I'm a religious person, and maybe, because of that, someone might say I believe in supernatural phenomena, and maybe they would be right. But I compartmentalize my own religious beliefs in a special exceptional category, and otherwise I tend to look at the world with a rational, scientific perspective - or at least I think I do. I don't believe in ghosts or the predictions of fortune tellers, and I don't have visions.

Maybe at times, I have had troublesome dreams where, for the life of me, I couldn't understand or explain why I had them. But then, I just shake my head, put it aside and don't let it bother me, and I go on with my life. I have never had the time nor the patience to bother with strange things I could not explain. There might be a scientific rationale for strange dreams and other strange happenings, but they don't affect my life, and I've never found it worth my while to delve into these things. But now, I have to deal with this deposition of Kate Lord, and I want to be sure I have the best understanding possible about what scientists would say about it."

Dr. Bezic smiled. "You sound pretty normal, Mr. Born. If we were to take a survey of the whole population of the country, they would say something similar, religious to some extent, but not putting much stock in extrasensory perception or clairvoyance. As a researcher and a clinical psychologist, I encounter all kinds of people with brains that seem to work in ways that are off the norm, sometimes way off. I don't laugh at any of them. I try to be a good listener, ask the right questions, and show some empathy and respect - something a lot of them don't get from a society of 'normal' people. The fascinating thing, to me, about Kate Lord, is that she seems to be otherwise very normal with some outstanding skills and can function perfectly well in society most of the time, but then . . . ," his voice trailed off. "But then she occasionally has these episodes that don't occur very often but impact her in such a way that she is ready and willing to make dramatic changes in her life, because she is confident that she has looked into the future and knows what is going to happen. She is making decisions against her objective self-interests, as well as against Constance's best interests. It seems she really believed her dreams. She doesn't sound like she's faking it. She really believes she has looked into the future and has seen, in advance, something terrible that is going to happen. It's very real to her."

"As a psychologist, how do you think a 12-person jury might react to her story?" Ted asked.

"Of course, that will depend on your jury and how you present and argue it," Bezic answered. "You obviously want a jury of hard-nosed practical people, people who work with their hands, like plumbers, or people who work with numbers, like clerks and accountants, married people with families. Avoid social workers and people who have dealt with dementia or other mental health problems in their families or with close friends. And then, I think you have to be careful to treat Kate with respect; you don't want your jurors to be offended that you are browbeating or ridiculing this poor woman who - rightly or wrongly - is sincere in her beliefs."

"Tell me what the scientific community thinks of these seers or people who claim to be clairvoyant. Are there any scientific studies of this kind of thing?" Ted Born asked.

"Yes, there have been all kinds of studies over the last century-and-a-half, including some at universities where I have studied or done advanced research. A study will come out every once-in-a-while that will seem to show that there might be some validity to some sort of psychic events, and then it will be followed by more rigorous studies with very careful controls that will show that the results correlate only with pure chance. Some people even bring quantum mechanics into the discussion, saying that some natural phenomena at the nuclear level are hard to explain logically and yet appear to be true. The bottom line is that there have been university programs and private interest groups who have examined these psychic phenomena for many, many years and have done a great many studies and experiments. So far, there is no good proof that anything is happening in the studied events other than simple random chance. Of course, there are anecdotal events that have been reported that are not subject to replication, and they remain unexplained, but they are not a reason to depart from the vast field of scientific research which shows that supernatural explanations are at least generally noncredible," Bezic answered.

"So, the oracle at Delphi probably accidentally foresaw the destruction of the Persian fleet by the Greeks at Salamis?" grinned Ted.

"If you notice, Ted, the oracle stories from Greek legends often did what fortune tellers today do - they answer ambiguously, or in a riddle that can be interpreted multiple different ways, and they hope the true facts that later occur can somehow get viewed in a way that fits the puzzle or riddle - not to mention the gas fumes the oracle was inhaling from the Delphic grounds!"

"I will need expert testimony at trial, Dr. Bezic. What would you be able to testify to at the trial?" Ted asked.

"Of course, I would like more details about the previous clairvoyant visions or dreams she says she has had, but I guess we are not going to be able to get that now, as you are expecting a fairly early trial. But I would say that, in any case, the scientific evidence is against the likelihood that the vision in her dream will ever come true. It was not something directed at Kate Lord, and there would be no reason to think Kate herself was in any danger. So, there was no reason to use this dream as a justification for abandoning her commitments to Constance, who she admits never did her wrong in any way. I would be entirely comfortable testifying along those lines," Bezic said.

"All right. I would like you to come aboard as an expert witness to provide just that kind of testimony, that the dream was probably no more than a dream and Kate herself was not a target of any harm, even if the dream was predictive of the future. And you would be prepared to go into scientific studies to justify your conclusions?" Ted asked.

"Yes, I am familiar with the leading studies, just need to brush up on some of the details before I testify. That should not take an especially long time. I will be ready," Bezic responded.

"All right. We'll keep in touch," Ted said.

Back in his office, Ted found an answer to the complaint filed by Zack Odom on behalf of Kate Lord. He began reading it and noted that there seemed to be no real disagreement as to the relevant facts. However, Zack had inserted some affirmative defenses, all of them centered upon Kate's contention she was justified in getting out of her contractual promises based on personal fear. First, the answer said there was an anticipatory breach of contract by Constance because Constance's lifestyle, coupled with the premonition of Constance's death meant that the contract was never capable of completion. Second, it was argued that Constance's lifestyle, coupled with premonition of Constance's death, could possibly have put Kate at risk for personal harm, that Constance's problems would inevitably spill over and endanger Kate, so Kate was justified in getting out.

"Amazing!" Ted said to himself. "These are the most far-fetched arguments I have ever heard. Anyway, if Kate had any concerns about her own personal safety or the prospects of carrying out the contract to completion, she had the obligation to call these reasons to Constance's attention and not just walk out on her. Zack had to use a lot of imagination to try to come up with a 'defense' this bad. Still, I wonder what he means about Constance's lifestyle. I guess I need to talk with Constance about that."

CHAPTER ELEVEN; Constance's Lifestyle

Jeremy had come in late from his office, and Connie had picked up some Chinese takeout food for dinner, which had gotten cold, so she warmed it up. Jeremy fixed a drink for himself and remarked to Connie, "I see you've already gotten yourself a drink, or is this your second or third one?"

"If you must know," Constance responded, "it is my second glass of wine. These are small glasses, and you have come home late again, so, yes, I'm not going to apologize. This is my second. So, what, are you monitoring me?"

"Connie, you are taking an opioid for back pain, probably too much of it. I don't deal with those drugs because I am a pediatrician, but I know that opioids and alcohol don't mix. They are very dangerous, long-range, for your liver, but short-term for all kinds of other risks. You really have to choose one or the other, not both," Jeremy said sternly.

"Jeremy, I am under a lot of stress, and my back pain is killing me. I'm not taking illegal drugs; the doctor has prescribed these pills. I know they don't do well with alcohol, but I take them late at night, just before going to bed, and early in the morning. I'm counting on the fact that they have cleared my system before early evening. I just can't give up a nice glass of wine or two around dinner time. I'm not going to do this forever, but right now I am under tremendous stress with the shop and the lawsuit and a lot of other things. I'm just trying to bridge myself to the other side of my troubles," Constance defended herself.

"This stuff you are taking is pretty new on the market, and I don't think the medical community has a really good handle on the dangers. As a pediatrician, I don't prescribe these drugs, and don't know a lot about them. I hear they all come from poppies, just like heroin, but it's said they are not as dangerous or as addictive as heroin. Still, you need to respect the potency of what you're taking, and especially be careful not to mix it with alcohol. You've changed in the last year or so, Connie. You are not yourself. You've always loved flowers, but you aren't making the floral arrangements like you used to. You rarely cook a meal for us. It's not good, and I know that damned shop is at the root of it, and there doesn't seem to be any solution," Jeremy lectured her.

"Well, what about you, Jeremy? You give me no support or even a word of sympathy. And you're supposed to be my husband, my safe place. You are hardly ever around, you come in late almost every night. I've found lipstick marks - not mine - on your shirts. I don't know whether it's that nurse in your office or someone else, but I need you, and I'm worried," Constance said, half accusing and half pleading.

"Let's just eat this Chinese stuff," Jeremy said non-responsively, and with a marble-cold face.

"And then maybe we can go to bed together? "Constance inquired suggestively.

"Maybe tomorrow," Jeremy responded. "I just need some plain sleep, old-fashioned as that might seem."

The next day, Constance was in Ted Born's office. "Constance, this answer to the complaint we have gotten from Kate's lawyer makes a reference to your 'lifestyle,' among other things, citing your lifestyle as a part of her excuse for running out on you. Of course, in the answer she also mentions the dream or vision she had of your demise. I expected that, but in her deposition, she made no reference to your lifestyle as having any relationship to her pulling out of the shop. It surprised me to see this 'lifestyle' issue cropping up in the answer. Have you got any idea what Kate and her lawyer are talking about?" Ted inquired.

Constance took a deep breath. Frankly, I don't know, Ted. She had seen me take some of my morning pills at times, and she knows I have a couple of glasses of wine with dinner - she doesn't drink at all, you know. Maybe she thinks I'm an addict, but she's never seen me in a position where I was impaired. I am just trying to cope, Ted, during a very difficult time, and I think I am coping, and it should be of no concern to her, as none of that affects her or her relationship at the shop."

"No run-ins at all between you and Kate?" he asked.

"Nothing," answered Constance. Then she added, "Well, she's probably heard me quarrel a bit with Jeremy when we talk on the telephone. It's a small office, and everyone can hear whatever is said one-way on the phone. I try to avoid conversations with Jeremy while at the office, and *always* when we have customers, but she's probably picked up on the fact that all is not perfect between Jeremy and me."

"I don't want to pry, Connie, and you don't have to answer or go into any details, but do you consider that things are really rocky in your marital relationships, at least to the extent that it is affecting your shop, and possibly could have affected your relationship with Kate?" Ted tried to ask politely.

"My relationship with Jeremy is not great right now, although I've tried to be careful to insulate the shop and my business from it. So, I don't see how it could have been of any concern to Kate, or to any of our employees. I might have said something to Kate, like 'Husbands!' in a tone of exasperation, but that would have been the extent of it. My problems with Jeremy all stem from the shop. Jeremy has his profession, and he has a life with his clients and professional friends, and he has a sense of worth and achievement in that way. And he doesn't understand why I don't just stay at home and arrange flowers and limit my outside life to my club meetings and the Junior League. But I have a desire to achieve something, to have people respect me for more than just being a socialite wife, to have clients like Jeremy does, who look up to me. I feel I am creative and artistic and have something to contribute, but unfortunately this shop venture has not turned out the way I planned. It's made my life more complicated and in some ways Jeremy's also, and at this point there is no easy way forward that I can see, beyond the lawsuit, of course," Constance answered, carefully choosing her words.

"I've learned nothing is perfect, and not many things are easy," Ted noted. "I hope this turns out to be just a bump in the road and that you can get past it and reestablish a good family life. I know you have two beautiful children. Life is never free of problems. We cannot avoid them; we eventually have to confront them. Unfortunately, when you confront them, you don't always win. We could lose this lawsuit, you know. Nothing is guaranteed. But I have learned that you can always be a winner if you don't let setbacks break your spirit. Don't ever give up, and don't let a lost battle keep you from continuing to fight for a life of fulfillment.

"In the meantime," Ted continued, "we should be able to prevent any lifestyle contentions from getting into the trial proceedings in your case against Kate Lord. She swore in her deposition that the only reason for her pullout from the shop was the premonition, the nightmare essentially that she had, of a bad end for you. And we will have some good expert testimony that such premonitions have no scientific basis and would not justify her abandonment of her contractual commitment. So, I think we are in a good situation legally, as much as we can be. Remember that some of those commitments in your paperwork were pretty vague and open-ended, and whether you win, and how big you win, are far from sure. We are just going to do the best we can and hope we have a good and reasonable jury."

CHAPTER TWELVE:
The Trial

The Court accommodated the parties, based on their mutual request, with an early jury trial, wedging them in where the Judge was confident one or more settlements by other litigants would open up a space. As a condition of getting the special setting, the Court wanted assurance that the trial would not extend beyond two days, and the parties agreed, subject to the length of jury deliberation, which everyone agreed was not likely to be very long.

Constance had a bit of a struggle deciding what to wear, being mindful of Ted's admonition to dress plainly, without flashy jewelry, and no scented perfume. Giving up the perfume was one of the hardest parts for Constance, as she felt positively naked without it, but she managed. She was not accustomed to dressing down. It had been decided that, on the day of trial, Constance would pick up Ted at his office, and she would drive to the Courthouse, and they would go in together to the Courtroom.

Constance's regular car was full of lace samples and other items when she went down to get in her car to pick up Ted, and she did not want to clear it out, and, besides, she thought Ted might be impressed by her replica car instead, a full-sized working model of a 1936 convertible classic car, painted in gleaming color in the crimson/maroon family. It was an adult "toy" she had arranged to be built from a kit to simulate the original model, although the engine under the hood had been updated to make driving easier and safer for the current generation. When she arrived in front of Ted's office, he was waiting on the sidewalk in accordance with their prearrangement. Ted's jaw dropped when he saw Constance pull up to the curb in this distinctive vehicle. Everyone on the sidewalk was equally interested and they began to walk toward the car and ask questions about it. Ted self-consciously got into the open convertible, told the interested spectators they were late for an appointment and could not stop to answer questions. Ted's first words to Constance were not those of a standard greeting, but, "Constance! I had no idea you had a car like this! Why did you drive it today?" All the while, gawkers on the sidewalks were straining to take it in as it passed them. A few of them, Ted's lawyer colleagues, smiled and waved at Ted.

"Well, Ted, it was clean and ready to go, and my other car was a mess. It's just a good, functioning car - there's one little problem at times - the steering is not quite right, but I think we'll make it to the Courthouse," Constance said, as though it was all "no-big-deal."

"I appreciate your coming by the office to pick me up, but, you know, we've been talking about maintaining a fairly low profile for you, no extravagant jewelry, little or no perfume. You were to project yourself as a plain housewife with a dream that Kate dashed. What if people on the jury venire see us parking and getting out of this car? They would think you were loaded with gold and riches, and it would destroy sympathy they might otherwise feel for you. I am going to suggest we park the car in a deck a couple of blocks farther from the Courthouse, rather than the usual one right nearby. My hope is that none of the potential jurors will see us arriving in the car. I don't want to make a big fuss out of this, but you have to avoid introducing an extraneous issue of wealth into the litigation, contrasting your wealth with Kate's. It shouldn't make any difference, because it is irrelevant to the legal issues, but jurors are human, and they have their biases, and we want to avoid fueling possibly adverse biases," Ted instructed her.

Ted directed her to a parking deck somewhat removed from the Courthouse, and he scanned the parking area to see if there were other persons around who would notice their exiting the convertible that stood out so conspicuously from all the other cars. Seeing no one, he and Constance quickly closed the cover, locked the car door, and walked toward the Courthouse. As they walked, Ted continued, "Connie, what did you mean about the steering being unreliable? That's pretty important, you know. Neither of us should be riding in a deathtrap, even if it is an enviable and gorgeous car."

"I wanted to be honest, Ted. Sometimes, the steering has not been responsive, and Jeffrey and I have to stop it and pull over and then gently start it again. We have had mechanics look at it, and I hope it's fixed now, but we don't take the car out on the road much, so I am not totally sure it has been fixed. It all worked fine this morning, but I thought I ought to alert you, just in case," Constance replied.

They spotted Kate and her lawyer, Zack Odom, as they approached the steps of the Courthouse, greeted each other with restrained politeness, and then entered the building and walked down the long corridor to the Courtroom. The room was beginning to fill with potential jurors who had been summoned for cases set for trial that week. Some of them had already begun jury service in other trials, but those not already selected for jury service were taking seats in the Courtroom, waiting to see if they would be serving on Constance's case, although they had probably never heard of Constance or Kate before entering the Courtroom that morning. They had all gone through the basic qualifying process to determine whether they were qualified to sit on juries in general, but they now needed to go through a further qualification process to determine if they could properly serve on this particular jury. It did not take long to do that, as none of them had ever heard of either of the parties and indicated no particular biases. Ted looked intently at each of the thirty jurors who made the cut to be potential jurors on Constance's case. The lawyers asked them a few questions to ferret out potential prejudice or backgrounds that might predispose them to favor one side or another. They seemed a fairly representative group. When the jury questioning was over, the attorneys on each side would have the chance to strike, one-by-one, jurors they preferred not to serve. Ted struck those less educated or unemployed, including a seamstress who, Ted thought, might identify with Kate. Ultimately, after the lawyers alternately struck potential jurors, there were twelve jurors and an alternate who remained and were said to have been "selected" to serve on the Constance/Kate jury, and they were sworn in and took their seats in the jury box.

After some general instructions and introductory comments by the Judge, it was time for opening statements, with Ted going first because he represented the plaintiff who had filed the lawsuit and who had the burden of proof.

"Ladies and gentlemen, this is not a complicated case. It really just comes down to whether a person who makes a promise is required to keep it, especially when someone else has relied on that promise and has gone out on a limb because of that promise. The question is whether it is wrong or legal for the person who made the promise to walk out on the partner who was depending on the promise being kept.

"In this case, my client, Constance Stanfield - often just called 'Connie' - and Kate Lord decided to open a shop that would specialize in selling lace and teaching customers how to sew and make best use of the lace. My client, Connie, agreed to bear all the expenses of setting up the shop, and she was going to give 40% - nearly half - to Kate who did not put one dime into the business. Connie even named the store after Kate, calling it "Katherine Lord's Laces." All Kate had to do was to teach a few classes and come in on flexible hours to meet and greet customers. There was potential for the shop to expand, like a franchise, starting with a person in

Charleston who wanted to explore opening a franchise in that city. It is important for you to understand that Kate's involvement was of critical importance to the store's success, because she had a reputation of being an expert on laces, while Connie was more or less a beginner. The store was opened, and for a few weeks, Kate did what she had promised to do, and it looked like the store was going to be a success. But then, Kate walked out on Connie and refused to participate any further. Strangely, Kate would not give any reason for her walkout, leaving Connie with a store that had a lot of potential, but without Kate the store seemed doomed to failure. You will hear from the evidence that Connie made every effort to talk with Kate and reason with her and find out what the problem was, if any. Kate still never would give any reason for her actions, just leaving Connie with a store on her hands that Connie would never have spent the money to open, without trusting Kate to keep her promise and to do her part. You will hear as a part of the evidence that Kate admits Connie never wronged her in any way and was always fair to her. Yet she left Connie in the lurch. We did not find out until AFTER this lawsuit was filed, when we were able to take Kate's deposition, that Kate says she had a dream that Connie would die, and that's why she walked out on Connie. A dream!!! Kate walked out on Connie because of a dream she had! And she had no other reason to do it. You will hear all this in the evidence, and we ask only that you listen carefully to the evidence, as I know you will, and ask yourself whether Kate wronged Connie, all under the instructions that the Judge will give you at the end of the case.

"I think I speak for all of us in the Courtroom that we appreciate your good service, because your service is all about maintaining our system of justice, which at times can seem very fragile, but it succeeds because of the service of good citizens like you. Thank you very much."

The Judge nodded to Zack Odom, and Odom rose to make his opening statement on behalf of Kate Lord. "Ladies and gentlemen,

I join Mr. Born in thanking you for your service here today. I will keep my remarks brief so that we can get on with the trial. I would like to stress that this 'agreement' Mr. Born referred to is vague and open-ended. It doesn't say how long my client has to be involved in this shop, for example. Would she be expected to be involved forever? It doesn't say how many classes she is required to teach, nor what her hours of work would be. So, we don't think there was ever a clear and defined contract in the first place. Second, no one but Kate can evaluate the trauma she felt when she had a vision of the future. Mr. Born pooh-poohs the dream she had of the bad ending to take pace at some point in the future according to Kate's dream. It was no laughing matter to Kate who sincerely believes that she is endowed with the ability to see the future at times, and Kate believes the reality of dreams that, to her, go beyond being mere dreams but are true visions of future events. And there was also a matter of a clash of lifestyles -"

Ted Born rose from his seat immediately, his hand raised, and said, "Your Honor, I object to the reference to 'lifestyles.' In Mrs. Lord's deposition I asked her if there was any reason for her quitting the project other than the dream, and she said 'No,' and I have the deposition right here. Mr. Odom should not be permitted to introduce other reasons that his client under oath has already disclaimed."

Zack Odom responded, "I withdraw the statement. It wasn't that important anyway." The Judge instructed the jury to disregard the reference to lifestyles. Then Zack continued, "Mrs. Stanfield has not been harmed. She still has her business, her shop. She still has the right to use Kate Lord's name in the name of her shop; she can continue calling it 'Katherine Lord's Laces.' Kate has given up her 40 per cent interest in the business. And she did help Connie get the shop up and running. Connie has gotten her money's worth out of Kate Lord, and she should be grateful for that and let Kate live out her life without continuing forever to be a part of an operation that frankly frightens her. We believe that when you hear the evidence you will agree that Kate Lord essentially fulfilled her part of the deal and was justified in withdrawing when she did. Thank you very much for your consideration."

The Judge then looked at Ted Born and said, "Mr. Born, please call your first witness."

Ted announced, "Your Honor, I call Katherine Lord as my first witness, and I would note that she is an adverse and possibly hostile witness," signaling to the Judge that Born might be asking some leading questions, that are permissible in the case of adverse parties or hostile witnesses. Zack Odom seemed taken aback, apparently having expected that Ted would probably call his own client Constance as his first witness. However, Ted felt he would have an advantage if the jury got its first impression of Kate as she responded to Ted's questions, rather than hearing her answer Zack's softball questions. Ted really did not have to lead her very much because her deposition had been very favorable to Constance's case, and Kate could scarcely argue with or deny her own prior deposition testimony.

When Ted got to the place where Kate said it was the dream of Constance's demise that caused her to abandon her partner and the project, Ted probed as to Kate's belief she was a seer. "Mrs. Lord, you say that you are a seer. Does that mean that every dream you have will definitely come true?"

"No, not every dream. It has to be a very vivid dream, and sometimes there are voices that speak to me about what I am seeing in the dream," Kate responded.

"Did you hear voices when you experienced your dream about Connie and her fate?" Ted asked.

Kate: "I heard voices, but they were muffled, and I couldn't make out what they were saying, except for one sentence, when the voices said, 'This is the ending.'"

Ted: "Wasn't it obvious that, in the dream, the death you saw of Connie was of course the end? The message from the voices was not necessary for you to know that - would you agree?"

Kate: "It wasn't so much what was said. It was the fact that there *was* a voice. Almost every time there has been an overlay of a voice, speaking like God, or something, I have found it is a true view of the future, a prophecy of things to come."

Ted: "How many of your dreams have turned out to be a true vision of things that actually did happen later?"

Kate: "Not so many serious or frightening ones. Some are of happy things, like gathering of family at a Thanksgiving dinner table, where what I saw in my dream actually turned out to be true, same people, dressed the way they were in my dream, and the same family member missing."

Ted: "How many dreams have you had, accompanied by voices, that were frightening, and that turned out to be true in real life later?"

Kate: "A few. I dreamed my dog went missing, and it later happened that my dog got loose and disappeared. I never knew what happened, and I had tried to watch the dog because of the dream, but it seemed like destiny had decided that it had to happen, and I couldn't stop it, no matter how careful I was. I dreamed my uncle in the Marines would die in combat in a foreign land, and it happened in World War II, and my father lost a fortune."

Ted: "Did you hear voices each time, in the case of your dog and your uncle?"

Kate: "I think so. It's been a long time. I can't remember the exact words. These dreams don't happen all the time, but when they do, something tells me, 'This is real,' not in those words, but in a way that I know these are not ordinary dreams but a vision of future events."

Ted: "Have you ever discussed these dreams or visions with a medical professional, such as a psychiatrist or a psychologist?"

Kate: "I once talked with a psychologist about it. He mainly listened and had no comments about it, except to say not to take them too seriously. He was not very understanding or supportive. But I don't need a psychologist to tell me anything about this. I know it's real, and I know I do need to take it seriously. I can't brush it off."

Ted: "It is not uncommon for dogs to get lost nor, sadly, for soldiers to die in battle in a war. Did it occur to you that these could have been coincidences, the occurrence of natural fears based on the reality that these were highly plausible possibilities in your mind before you ever had your dreams?"

Kate: "The thought occurred to me that it could have been a coincidence, but the vision was very vivid, and most dogs do not get lost, and most soldiers don't die in battle."

Ted: "Let us suppose for a moment that your dream about Constance Stanfield might come true at some future time. How would that knowledge hurt you now - today - to such an extent you would feel you had to cut off your relationship with her?"

Kate: "I'm an emotional person. I couldn't work with her, knowing something terrible might happen to her at any time."

Ted: "Wouldn't it have been the kind and considerate thing to do, to stay with her and be as supportive and comforting as possible?"

Kate: "It might be kind to her, if I had nerves of steel, but I am emotionally fragile."

Ted: "Once again, assuming that Constance's end was as you dreamed, did you stop to think that your abandonment of her might speed up the time when the dream would come true?"

Kate: "I never thought of it that way. To me, her fate was written on a wall somewhere, and it was going to happen, regardless of what I did. I just knew I needed to get out of that situation."

Ted: "How many of these dreams have you had that have come true, at least the ones that frightened you?"

Kate, beginning to sob: "There have been others. I don't want to get into them. I just can't do it."

Ted: "You are not going to get into them when Mr. Odom asks you questions, are you?"

Kate: "God, no, surely he won't ask me. I just can't do it."

Ted: "Let's move on, then. You understood, did you not, when you and Kate made your deal, that you were to participate for a lot longer than you did?"

Kate: "Well, until the shop was established and doing well."

Ted: "And, just to be sure, Mrs. Lord, Connie was never unfair to you, never insulted you or made your job burdensome to you, and you were never subject to any insults or abuse by any of the customers?"

Kate: "I have to say that's all true. That's not why I left, not why I felt I had to leave."

Ted: "And the shop had barely opened. It was a long way from being established and doing well, wasn't it?"

Kate: "Yes, but I thought the hardest part was behind us, just getting the store opened, and I helped with the opening and some follow-up."

Ted: "Mrs. Lord, why did you not extend the courtesy to Constance to go and talk with her and explain why you were getting out, and try to work out some reasonable transition?"

Kate: "It wouldn't have changed anything. I didn't want to get in an argument with her. I was determined to leave immediately, and nothing could change that."

Ted: "Even if such a conversation did not change your mind, did it occur to you that the kind thing to do would be to explain the situation to Constance and not leave her wondering why you left her in the lurch?"

Kate: "I didn't think she would understand, better just to leave and have a clean break."

Ted: "But it was in fact not a clean break at all when you left with no notice or explanation. Do you understand that now?"

Kate: "I just don't know how to answer that."

Ted concluded his questioning and tendered the witness to Zack Odom. Odom began by asking Kate about the vagueness of the documents she and Connie signed in setting up the business. Kate answered, "Well, we didn't have it all nailed down, but we trusted each other." Zack asked her if she sincerely believed her dream would become reality, and Kate said, "Yes."

Then Zack asked how the dream affected her in her relationship to the shop. Connie said, "I was terrified. I just couldn't continue. I didn't know what I had stepped into, but I was afraid, afraid for Connie and afraid I might be involved if I stayed on as Connie's partner." Zack had no other questions.

Ted had one additional question: "Mrs. Lord, you have just testified that all the details of your partnership relationship had not been spelled out fully, but that you each trusted each other. However, do you still agree with your testimony when I was questioning you, that you knew you were supposed to stay with the business and do your part at least until the business was well established?"

Kate: "Yes, I have to agree I knew that."

Ted: "And do you also agree that the business of the shop was far from 'established' when you left?"

Kate: "I more or less agree that it still had a long way to go, although it had made progress."

Ted decided not to press that point any further, and Zack had no more questions, so the witness was excused from the stand, but was to remain in the courtroom. Ted then called Dr. Bezic to the stand. After establishing Dr. Bezic's status as an expert witness, Ted asked Bezic to describe the current state of the scientific view of the relationship of dreams as a predictor of reality to come.

Dr. Bezic testified, "There have been many studies at distinguished universities, going back to Sigmund Freud, and the consensus of those studies is that dreams are not reliable portrayals of future reality. There have been anecdotal incidents where someone would have a dream and it would be followed by something similar in real life, but when studied under controlled conditions, the studies invariably show that such incidents are accidental coincidences. We have no documented scientific studies, under scientifically controlled conditions, that find any foretelling of the future in dreams. Fortunately for us, we don't have to rearrange our lives because of something we dreamed that might disturb us."

Ted: "Doctor, I take it you are referring to studies of the population as a whole, but are there scientifically documented individuals who have special powers to foresee the future through dreams?"

Bezic: "Actually many of the studies I referred to were undertaken precisely because certain persons claimed to have the power to foresee the future, and studies were set up to determine whether they could indeed foresee the future through their dreams. It turns out that, when the dreams of such persons are studied over an appropriate period of time, and then those dreams are checked to see if they come true, it turns out that no one has been found who has such clairvoyant powers. Now, we all understand that sometimes dreams are connected to events that are taking place in our lives, and some of those events can take only one of two possible paths. Obviously, in that particular and limited circumstance, there is a 50% possibility that the resolution suggested by the dream will play out in real life, but that is not based on clairvoyance; it is based on a statistically expected outcome due to the specific circumstances."

Dr. Bezic went on to comment on Kate's dream and its significance relative to clairvoyance: "Here, Mrs. Lord was only tangentially involved in the private life of Mrs. Stanfield, and only through a business relationship. Her dream about Mrs. Stanfield's demise is very vague and did not involve Mrs. Lord except as an accidental observer. It is very unlike a dream that occurs when someone is wrestling with a problem personal to him or her and where there is bound to be a resolution one way or another. Here, Mrs. Lord had a dream that does not appear to have been connected to any unresolved issues with which she was struggling in her personal life, just something that popped up and she happened to observe it. I do not attach any clairvoyant value to Mrs. Lord's dream."

Ted: "Dr. Bezic, Mrs. Lord appears to believe she is clairvoyant, whether she is or is not. Would she have a reasonable enough concern in her own mind to base her continued participation in the lace shop solely on her belief the event she dreamed about was going to occur in real life?"

Bezic: "I cannot address the genuineness of Mrs. Lord's concerns in her own mind, but I can say that there was no reasonable basis for her to discontinue her participation in the lace shop based on her dream."

Ted's next witness was a CPA accountant who calculated a range of damages Constance sustained as a result of Kate's walking out on her, based on the monetary investment, income and profit expectations, damage to goodwill, and loss of franchising opportunities.

Ted finally called Constance as his final witness, who graphically, and occasionally tearfully, recounted her traumatic predicament. He had no other witnesses, and Zack did not elect to call any, stating that his client Kate had already provided all testimony relevant to her position. It was time for the closing arguments. Ted Born went first:

"Ladies and gentlemen, as trials go, this has been a fairly short one, but I ask you not to judge its importance by its length. To the real people involved, this trial is of crucial importance because its outcome can affect their lives and their futures in profound ways. My client, Connie Stanfield, put not only all the money she had, and a lot that was borrowed, to fulfill a dream she had of a shop that would be different, a shop that would add a new dimension of beauty to those who could learn at her shop how to make beautiful clothes for children in styles you can't buy off the shelves, but nicer, harkening back to an earlier time when people made the effort and devoted themselves to creating beautiful handmade clothes. We have lost the will and the desire to make these beautiful creations, and Connie wanted to set up this special shop to spread the knowledge and preserve and foster interest in this almost lost art.

"Connie herself was somewhat new to this revelation of how beautiful clothes could be, especially for small children, and she went to the lady who had become her mentor, full of excitement, with the idea of a special shop to showcase lace and how to create beautiful things with lace; she went to Kate Lord and proposed this shop, and Kate was enthusiastic as well. They would plan their shop and stock it; they would have displays of beautiful clothes; they would have kits to make sewing easier, and they would give sewing classes. Kate was not willing or able to contribute money to set up the shop, but Connie agreed to take on the responsibility for rounding up the money, and she would give Kate 40% of the profits and would even name the store after Kate. Each of them would help with the opening of the shop, the open houses, and they would greet customers and advise them and teach classes. This was a partnership, and partnerships do not generally have a specific duration. But partnerships are based on mutual promises that each party will uphold his or her part of the program, and Connie went out on a limb and relied on Kate's promise to do her part to make this partnership a success.

"Now, with Connie out on this limb, Kate had a dream that at some point in the future Connie would meet an untimely death. There was nothing in the dream that was a threat to Kate. And yet Kate says she was afraid to stay with the program and just walked out on Connie. She never even did Connie the courtesy of explaining why in the world she had just suddenly quit, leaving Connie to pick up the pieces - and the impossible job of putting them back together again. Kate was adamant she would never come back, and she would not talk with Connie or give her any clue as to why she had walked out. In fact, it was only after Connie felt compelled to file this lawsuit that Kate, in a deposition with a Court reporter present, told Connie why she had walked out. It is possible that, in her own mind, Kate felt she should break away even though the cause of the break was only a dream. But people have responsibilities to each other that cannot just be brushed away because of a bad dream. Connie had a right to rely on Kate's promises, and Connie had a right to expect Kate to act reasonably. You have heard the testimony of our expert witness psychologist who testified that Kate's reaction to her dream was not a reasonable one, that there is no scientific evidence that seers or fortune tellers can really see the future through dreams. Kate's drastic action must be looked at through the lens of Connie's reasonable expectations, based on mutual promises and partnership relationship and NOT on Kate's unreasonable interpretation of her dream. We look with compassion on Kate or anyone who would act as Kate has, but we cannot ignore the harm that has been done to another innocent person - Connie. We respectfully ask you to do justice for Connie and compensate her in full for her loss. She will have a tough road ahead of her, but this compensation will help. Thank you for your careful attention to the evidence in this trial, which is so important to everyone concerned."

Zack Odom then rose and addressed the jury. "Ladies and gentlemen, I too thank you for your service, and I just wish to remind you of several things to bear in mind. First, it was not Kate's idea to start this shop; it was Connie's idea, and she talked Kare into going along with it. Kate contributed her name and her reputation to the effort to get the shop going, which was an important contribution to its success. She met with customers, and she taught classes, and she did her part as long as she felt she could. She would have continued except for an unanticipated development that threw a monkey wrench into the project - the vision of an unfortunate end for her partner. Now, the plaintiff can make light of this if she wishes, but Kate sincerely believed that she had seen a vision of what was to come, and she felt she could not continue. But she did the right thing. She didn't just walk away; she gave up her 40% interest in the project, even though she had already done a great deal to help out with Connie's project. She willingly surrendered her substantial ownership interest, which she felt was compensation to Connie. Kate is entitled to a lot of credit. She was helpful and conscientious, and she has refused to criticize or say anything ill of Connie. Surely, Kate has a right to make decisions that she felt she needed to make to preserve her physical and mental wellbeing. Kate was in fear of her own safety, and anyone who has any compassionate feelings should understand Kate's dilemma and applaud the fair manner in which she broke off the relationship when she felt she had to do that. We ask that you put this matter in perspective and recognize that justice has already been done if you leave these two ladies where they are now - Kate with her freedom and Connie with her business. Thank you for your attention and consideration."

Then it was Ted's turn for rebuttal. "Ladies and gentlemen, let me set the record straight a bit. Nobody twisted Kate's arm to get her into this partnership with Connie. Yes, Connie came up with the idea, but Kate was also enthusiastic about it. Second, it was Connie, not Kate, who invested the money necessary to make this shop possible, and Connie generously gave her a 40% interest in it without it costing her a cent. Connie took 100% of the financial risk, but generously gave Kate nearly half of potential profits and value. Ask yourselves whether anyone would have been so generous if she had known Connie would walk out on her before the business had been securely established. Obviously, not. Yes, Kate did come to the store and interact with customers in the beginning, and she taught a few classes in sewing with lace, but she got paid for doing that. She didn't make a free contribution of her time and efforts. She got paid for it, over and above the 40% interest Connie gave her. I submit to you that a promise is a promise. Kate made a promise to Connie that she did not keep. Our whole society is dependent on the proposition that people ought to be held to their promises. We can't function if people are allowed to disavow their promises merely because they had a bad dream. If that were so, anybody could walk away from their obligations at any time by claiming they had a bad dream. Our whole system of contracts would collapse if that were so. And, I see my rebuttal time is expiring, but I would remind you that, when Kate walked out on Connie and left her holding the bag, she would not respond to Connie's request that they discuss restoring their relationship and would not even give Connie a clue as to why she had walked out. It was handled in a very cruel and unfeeling manner. My rebuttal time is up, but I ask you to award Connie the full measure of damages to which our expert witness testified. Thank you."

The Judge thanked counsel and gave standard charges to the jury and sent them into the jury room to deliberate. Ted and Constance went out to get some fresh air and a change of scenery. Constance looked at Ted and said, "Well, Ted, I thought what you said sounded good to me, but what do you think?"

"Connie, I thought the jury was taking in some of what Zack was saying, and it bothered me. I tried to answer what I thought might have been some questions in the jury's minds, and I thought I was getting through to some of them, but the dynamics of a jury, when they go into deliberations, are hard to predict. I tend to think the jury has some sympathy with the mental turmoil Kate says she experienced, but I also tend to think that they felt the turmoil was overblown or unrealistic and that you should not be made to suffer because of a kind of phobia that Kate seems to have. I guess we will soon have an answer."

In time, the bailiff came to the parties and announced, "The jury has a verdict." The parties returned to the courtroom and stood respectfully as the jury entered and took their seats in the jury box. The jury verdict form was handed up to the Judge from the foreperson, and the Judge read from the form: "We the jury find for the plaintiff and against the defendant, in the amount set forth below." The amount indicated was exactly what Constance's expert witness had testified to. Connie smiled at Ted and squeezed his hand. The jury was polled, and they stuck by their verdict. Judge Higgins thanked the jury and announced to the parties that he was entering judgment in accordance with the jury verdict.

Kate had tears in her eyes that she was wiping away with a lace handkerchief. Constance walked over to Kate and said, "I am truly sorry, Kate, that it came down to this. I didn't know what else to do. I know you have been through some anguish, and I have also. I wish it could have been avoided. I still think fondly of you."

Kate nodded, but she said nothing to Constance. The parties left with their attorneys.

When Constance and Ted returned to Ted's office, in Ted's car this time, not the replica, Constance asked, "Where do we go from here, Ted?" He told her that they would have to wait to see if Kate appealed the verdict, as the judgment could not be collected until the time for appeal ran out. He told her Kate would have to post a sizable bond if she wished to avoid paying the judgment pending appeal. He explained that, in the meantime, he expected Zack Odom to approach him with an offer in compromise to avoid an appeal. Meanwhile, Constance could take some satisfaction in having been vindicated, and now she would not feel constrained to wear plain attire and avoid strong perfume!

CHAPTER THIRTEEN:
Back at Helicon Heights

"So, you won your lawsuit. I guess I should break out the Champagne and celebrate, but I don't happen to have any handy. Where do you go from here?" Constance's husband Jeremy queried.

"I don't know, Jeremy. I have a lot of thinking to do, and I am just beginning to unwind," Constance answered.

"Well, you need to think it through. My guess is, you won't get the full amount of the judgment. They will come to you and negotiate it down, or, worse, Kate could go bankrupt on you, and you might not get anything," Jeremy speculated.

"Oh, I don't think she'll go bankrupt. I think I will get something monetarily, and at least I think my friends will be supportive, now that I have been found to be in the right," Constance replied.

"Connie, I don't think your 'friends' are going to give a damn, one way or the other. To them, this is just your problem. It's just all about a small store. You might think they have their antennas out, waiting breathlessly for any news about you and your lawsuit, but they really don't care. It might be worth a little gossip fodder, but that's all. As for the money from your jury verdict, how much are you going to have to pay Ted Born? That's going to eat into your recovery. Between whatever you get out of a compromise settlement and the amount you will have to pay Born, my guess is you are going to be left with just a fraction of what you need to break even. And you and your dad will still have an albatross around your necks. You'd better be thinking how you can offload that bird," said Jeremy.

"I have reported all this to Dad, and he seems very pleased. He knows there's still a lot that needs to be sorted out, but he is sympathetic and understanding and wants to be a part of a solution," Constance said with assurance, but thinking to herself, "I just wish I had a husband who would show some empathy and positivity. No matter what I do, he seems so negative."

"Jeremy, could you sometimes say something positive, something to show you are on my side? I try to be supportive of your medical practice and the strange and uncertain hours it demands of you. I was looking at this jury win as something that would maybe get us on the right track, re-establish the relationship we once had. Can't we fall in love again?" Constance implored Jeremy.

"Connie, maybe we ought to have this conversation at a later time. You've changed, and maybe I've changed. Let's both think about what we can do, if anything, to put our lives back together again. I can see that you have a lot of things to work out connected with your shop. Let's give you some time to focus on that, and then let's try to fall in love again. If we say those words tonight, they are just words. If we get things worked out so there is a clear path to the future, then we can say those words with the assurance that they are meaningful," Jeremy responded.

"Jeremy, are you saying we can't even make love again until all our financial and business issues are worked out? Some of those issues are difficult and will take some time. Do we have to put our personal lives on hold until everything is perfect? You didn't use to think, or act, that way. Jeremy, look at me and tell me whether there is somebody else in your life that has your focus right now," Connie said emphatically.

"See there, Connie, that's why I said we should have this conversation later. I knew it would degenerate into suspicions and accusations if we got into it now. You need to trust me, like I trust you," Jeremy parried the question.

"But. Jeremy, you haven't found someone else's lipstick on my blouse, and I don't come home late at night for unexplained reasons. Trust should be a two-way street all right, but what if it changes to a one-way thoroughfare? We have two beautiful children. Don't they and their mother mean anything to you?" Constance pleaded.

"There you go, bringing the children into this. Our problems are between you and me. Please leave the children out of it," Jeremy countered.

"Jeremy, I can't leave the children out of it. We are a family. We are together in this thing called life. What each of us does affects all of us. Think about it, and let's be loyal to each other, and do our darnedest to show our love and respect for each other. The children pick up on these things, you know, when Mama and Daddy aren't getting along. That's why I can't leave them out." It seemed at least for a moment that Jeremy was listening to Constance.

"Okay, Connie. You are right that I, and maybe each of us, needs to take stock of our priorities, and family ought to be at the top for both of us. How about, let's go to bed?" Jeremy asked with a smile.

"I thought you'd never ask! Takes a while for you to take a hint!" said Constance. They shared a brief hug and retired to their bedroom for the evening.

CHAPTER FOURTEEN:
Two Weeks Later

Two weeks had passed since the trial, and Ted had not been contacted by Zack Odom about resolving the case without an appeal. Constance had been nervous, almost as nervous as she had been before the trial. She felt she had to talk with Ted and gave him a call.

"No word yet from Zack?" Constance asked.

"Nothing," answered Ted. "It reminds me of the time before trial. We kept waiting for Zack to contact us about settling the case without a trial, but I never heard anything. Seems like the second verse of the same song. I assume you haven't heard anything directly from Kate, either? You know, she might give you a call. There would be nothing unethical about that. Parties can talk directly with each other without involving their lawyers if they wish. Sometimes they decide they can work things out without the help or expense of a lawyer, and that would be fine with me. From what I have seen of Kate, it's unlikely she would call you direct, as I gather she just really doesn't want to talk with you. To her, that dream makes you poison, and she doesn't want to associate with you in any way. So, if we hear anything, it probably will come through Zack, although he likewise will never be known as 'the great communicator.' However, his problem is that, if he does not communicate and get things worked out, his time for appeal will be running out, and I can't see him wanting an appeal, and I certainly don't see him opting to allow the judgment to become final without an appeal or settlement. So, he's got a couple of weeks, but this is not one of those things you would want to put off to the last minute, because time is running out on him. Of course, I could call Zack to try to feel him out as to whether he's going to appeal, but I don't think that would be good psychology on our part, because it would signal to him that we are fishing for a compromise settlement, and he would be encouraged to think he might be able to get a low settlement number from us. I think we just need to wait; it won't be too much longer, although I know you want to get this behind you."

"You are right that I want it resolved, and I should add that Jeremy seems very insistent that it be resolved. I've been thinking a lot about my situation, and I have a problem seeing a path to my future. I am assuming that, whatever the resolution to the lawsuit, assuming there is one, I am not going to come out whole, considering my capital investment - which, you know, is mainly from money Dad lent me. Considering the fact that I am operating at a loss every month, hoping for a breakeven that seems like a distant mirage, and considering the expense of litigation, I realize I am still going to be in a negative position and will still have the shop on my hands, piling up additional losses as far as I can foresee. What do I do then? I'll still have the money-losing albatross around my neck indefinitely, or I have to find a purchaser or go bankrupt. Finding a purchaser of a specialty money-losing business, where there are virtually no obvious prospects, is very unlikely. Bankruptcy would be embarrassing to me, and I don't think Jeremy would stand for it. Dad might forgive me, but I am reluctant to go to him and explain that I have thrown away his good money on a business which, frankly, has been a nightmare. I am trying to look ahead for a way out, and it doesn't look to me like I have any good options. Do you have any suggestions or thoughts about my dilemma?" Constance probed.

"Constance, I am a lawyer, not a distressed business adviser, so I am not sure I have much to offer. But I am sympathetic to your plight and have seen other clients who have worked their way out of a hole. I would first urge you to look beyond the horizon you see right now. For example, if you can't think of anyone who would be a prospective purchaser of your business *in its present format*, try to think of how it could be of value to someone in a modified form. I wonder if a department store would like to set up a specialty department in their stores specializing in this lace culture and would pay well for your reputation, expertise, and inventory. Or could the business be transformed so that it would extend beyond lace and increase your market reach? You know much more about lace and your particular business than I do, and you might know of possibilities that would not even occur to me. I just urge you to think outside the box. Some kind of transformation might require additional capital as well as sweat equity, but, if the concept is sound and would lead to profitability, the capital should be obtainable," Ted suggested.

"Those are good thoughts, Ted. But remember, I have two small children and a husband, and my husband did not like my present venture. I doubt he would put up with more of what he would call adventures or pipe dreams. Still, you have given me something to think about. I've been fixated on the business I have set up and am familiar with, and I haven't had much time or encouragement to think outside the box," Constance said.

"You know the old saying, though: if fate gives you lemons, make lemonade. You do have a concept that is not a run-of-the-mill type of business, and somewhere there should be value in that concept that maybe you could nourish. I can imagine that Jeremy would prefer for life to go back to the way it was before you got into opening a lace boutique, but surely he would not want you to make foolish or costly decisions now just to get rid of the business. Surely, he would find the patience to see you through this challenge you will be facing," Ted advised.

"I would have once agreed with that, but Jeremy is different now. He's changed, and he has zero empathy or sympathy for me and this lace project, as I have told you. He just wants me out of it. I'm not even sure our relationship would go back to normal, even if I was able miraculously to resolve all my problems instantly, by waving a magic wand. I know you are not a marriage counselor any more than you are a distressed business adviser, but you need to know, in connection with any lawsuit settlement or future plans after the lawsuit has been resolved, that I do have to confront problems in my marital relations, and I will have to factor that in as we go forward."

Ted responded, "You say 'as we go forward,' but I have been assuming I was hired just to handle this lawsuit. Are you saying you anticipate a role for me as your legal adviser after the lawsuit has gone away?"

"Of course, Ted," Constance replied emphatically. "I cannot imagine not having access to your counsel and advice from here on out. I want you to be my lawyer under any and all circumstances. I have never found anyone else who can look at a problem and take it apart piece-by-piece and analyze it wisely and objectively, like you can. Please tell me you will still be my lawyer!"

"I would be honored, Constance. You have my full professional loyalty. Now, let's hope the lawsuit resolution will come about soon, so we can at least get that behind you, and perhaps that will make your situation clearer. I am sure we will be in touch again shortly. So long," Ted assured Constance as they finished their call.

CHAPTER FIFTEEN:
The Shop Consumes Constance

Constance spent much of the following weekend at home, sitting on a couch in the den with a throw cushion at her back, looking through a stack of magazines dealing with fashions, home designs, and living décor trends. Ted had settled the lawsuit against Kate on a basis better than she expected, but the net proceeds she received were not going to sustain the boutique's operations for long, and, anyway, she had lost her enthusiasm for running it indefinitely until it reached profitability, which very likely was not going to happen on any reasonable timeframe. She also had spoken with friends, and with one broker in the business of marketing going concerns, and she had gotten no encouragement that a disposition of the shop was likely on any basis other than as a distress sale. She had hoped the lady in Charleston who had inquired about a possible franchise might be willing to buy the shop, but her interest was strictly limited to the Charleston area, with no interest in a Greenville shop. So, she decided to try making "lemonade" out of this boutique "lemon" she had on her hands, as Ted had suggested. Constance had taken the day off from the shop, and the nanny had taken the children to the playground, giving her some uninterrupted time to turn page-after-page of magazine-after-magazine, looking for inspiration.

Jeremy had been pressing her about her next step, and her dad had politely, but patiently, made inquiries as well. At this point she had no good answers. Lace could be applied to a lot of things besides children's clothing, like curtains, throw pillows, and even certain Victorian chairs, but it all required a lot of work - a lot of hand sewing - that most people had no time or patience to do. She wondered if she could convince a manufacturer to pay her for some of her design ideas, but most of the major companies had their own designers and, after all, Constance had no patents or even trademarks she could offer as value. Even for a good idea, manufacturers would normally pay only nominal sums for unpatented and unpatentable ideas. She did not see any good solutions, and her magazines were not giving her any positive inspiration. She was beginning to hate the situation in which she found herself. She could not bear to go to her father and say, "Dad, I have made a mess with this business idea you financed, and now I just have to liquidate and bankrupt the business, and I am afraid you will have to absorb the loss because I do not have the ability to pay you back as I expected and promised." She knew the stock market was not doing well, and she strangely had only vague notions of her dad's resources, never wanting him to think she was looking for an early inheritance. To her it had always been enough to feel that there was always money there if she needed it badly enough. But now she was wondering just how thick the professor's billfold really was, and how lenient his patience might be.

Constance went to her medicine cabinet and dispensed two prescription pills, one for anxiety and one for pain. She held them in her hand, looked at them and considered putting them back. She had earlier questioned her regular usage of these medications, and had quit using them, but she had kept them on hand, just in case. Now she decided it would help to take some because she had encountered nothing but dead ends in her search for solutions to her business and personal problems, promising herself that she would not make a habit of relying on them. After a while she still had no solutions, but she felt a sense of serenity that was comforting. Just then she got a call from her shop advising that a key salesperson had not shown up for work and she was needed there. "Lord, another headache, and I had counted on and was enjoying a rare break from the shop," she told herself. But dutifully, she left a note for the nanny, drove to the shop, and prepared to try to function as a cheerful salesperson. By the time she got there, the traffic into the store had dwindled to occasional browsers and just a trickle of serious customers, hardly worth the effort on Constance's part to be there. "There is more and more of this kind of thing that will be happening," Constance mused. "If I am going to have a shop, I have to keep the doors open during regular hours, and even if I have hired and am paying employees, I will never be able to count on any time at all that I can call my own. Maybe if I had a platoon of employees, I could act as a laid-back CEO and come and go as I please, but it would be years, if ever, before I could ever be in that situation. I've created a monster that has me by the throat and won't let me go. I'm miserable, and I don't know what to do."

Constance drove toward home, stopping at a gourmet meals-to-go place to pick up some sustenance for dinner that evening, then arrived at home to be greeted by two excited children and a polite nanny who was ready to go to her own home. "I guess this makes it all worthwhile," Constance told herself. "I'm not the best of mothers, though I want to be, but the children think I'm perfect. How I love them!"

She was feeding them supper in the breakfast room when Constance heard Jeremy's car enter the garage. Jeremy walked by Constance and patted the children on their heads, as they happily cried out, "Daddy! Daddy! Daddy's home!"

"See how they adore you, Jeremy! They are so excited to see you, and I am, too. Glad you got home a little earlier tonight than you sometimes do," Constance said.

"What's for dinner, Connie? Hopefully not chicken salad from the deli kiosk at the grocery store," Jeremy inquired.

"Well, it's not homemade, Jeremy, as I had to spend the afternoon at the shop. One of the employees called in sick, and, unfortunately, I had to go, even though I had programmed myself some time away from the shop. But I do have some beautiful veal chops with herbs and a nice white sauce, with broccoli –" Constance began.

"You know I don't like broccoli. How about some potatoes?" Jeremy interrupted.

"Yes, there are some home-style French fries that also came with the order, which I understand are fantastic. And, if you want some greenery, I can certainly make you a salad, with your choice of my homemade dressing or some chunky blue cheese dressing," Constance responded. "You will notice, the dining room table is set, and we can light the candles and make it a special dinner."

"So, you had to go to the shop today, did you? Is there ever going be a resolution that will free you from that damned shop?" Jeremy said with condemnation and disgust.

"I'm doing everything I can to arrive at what you call a 'resolution.' I've tried to sell the shop, without success so far. In the meantime, I can't just let the shop fade away into bankruptcy. To have any chance of selling it, it has to be a going business, with some promise, if the right management is in place. I am even looking at the possibility of a conversion of the store to something else to make it more marketable, hopefully something related and complementary, but I haven't found the right fit yet. I am still looking, of course, and I feel that something will turn up. Please don't tell me I never should have gotten into this. Of course, I know now that it was a mistake, but only because of something unknowable - that crazy dream Kate had. Who could have anticipated that? But I've been chastised enough about that, and I have chastised myself most of all. Still, I cannot go back and undo what has happened. I have to deal with it, and I need your moral support - not asking for any money, just a little empathy and understanding. Please bear with me and give me that!" Constance pleaded, almost in tears.

"Not sure how to give you moral support when you don't want my advice or judgment. I never thought the shop was a good idea, but you went ahead with it, and now it affects both of us," Jeremy responded. "By the way, have you been popping pills today to help deal with the stress of the shop?"

"I took a couple. I've tried to stay away from them but today was tough, and I felt I needed them. It would help a lot if you would just show me some love and affection and be considerate. With that, I think I can make it through this dismal swamp. That's all I want, your loyalty to me, just as I am loyal to you. Let's make a commitment that we will never let this, or any other external thing, come between us. The reason I keep wrestling with this shop issue on my own, and don't bring you into it in any direct way, is not that I don't value or want your advice; it's just that I know you are busy with your practice, and I don't want my troubles to impact your professional work. Of course, I know it's mainly my responsibility, not yours, and I am trying to shield you from my problems. Believe me, I want our relationship to endure, and much more," Constance explained.

"Let's take it day by day, Connie. We will just keep assessing our relationship and the shop problem. Let's hope you find a way out of the shop. That would go a long way." Jeremy prescribed clinically.

CHAPTER SIXTEEN:
Sorting Things Out

Constance was at the shop talking with a customer, Doris Hamrick. "Connie, I love your shop, and I love lacy children's clothes. But frankly, I just don't have time to do the sewing myself. I'm working three days a week, and I am trying to earn some credits toward my M.A. degree, and I have a family. It seems like I'm always ferrying the children to one thing or another - you know, group this and group that. And my husband Fred and I are trying to have a life at the same time. I would love to make a hobby out of this hand sewing, but I can't fit it in. It is fun but tedious, and when I do have a spare moment, the easiest thing is just to turn on the television. I just find myself taking the path of least resistance, and sewing doesn't fit that bill. I want somebody else to do the sewing right now, and I'll just enjoy seeing the children dressed in stunning outfits that someone else has made!" Doris announced with resignation.

"Doris, I hear the same thing over and over from customers. Learning the techniques of the fine hand sewing and trying your hand at it is a good and rewarding idea, but then other things crowd it out. They hope to get back to it sometime, but that gets pushed off into the future, and then the children are teenagers and wouldn't be caught in lacy clothes for the world. I'm glad there are some exceptions - people who somehow work the sewing into their schedule, but I've got to say, I hear an awful lot of just what you're telling me. You know, this shop started out as a kind of mission project, to spread the word about sewing with lace, but I've learned that there are limits to what my customers can fit into their schedules, and I do need customers to keep the shop going," Constance confessed.

"Maybe there is a way to broaden your market," Doris suggested. "I heard something that seems crazy to me, but you might look into it. I read or heard somewhere that someone or some company had developed a synthetic lace, looks real but is polyester, and - get this - it can either be sewed onto other fabric or even ironed onto some fabrics. You apparently just take a hot iron and iron a border of the lace onto the edge of certain other fabrics. It apparently doesn't work - the iron-on - with all fabrics. You couldn't iron it onto corduroy, for example, but you could do it on organdy or many synthetic materials. This would make it easy to add lace to curtains or throw pillows, and maybe certain furniture fabrics - wherever the ironed-on border could be concealed and where the lace is not likely to be examined too carefully. You probably wouldn't want to use it on lacy children's clothes, but it could broaden your market by bringing into the shop people who like the look but cannot or don't want to do hand sewing on other things. Think about it."

"Sounds interesting, Doris. I don't know whether there would be too much of a culture clash to bring ersatz lace into a shop founded to further the art of hand sewing, but it's worth looking into, I guess. I am really out of other ideas. Got any information about whom I might contact about this?" Constance asked.

"Not offhand. But I will see if I can think back where I learned about this, and I will give you a ring, if I find out anything. Okay, here's my credit card for my purchases. I need to be on my way," Doris said.

Constance pondered the new type of lace after Doris had left the store. "It all seems crazy to me," Constance thought. "I wonder if this is just experimental and will never be actually marketable. I've never heard of it, and, anyway, I can't see how I could mesh this machine-made material with selling real lace whose essence is authenticity. Anyway, I need to be thinking of how I can extricate myself from the business, not expand and complicate things."

However, Doris called Constance a few days later, providing her with contact information. It seemed some individuals had come up with a process for making synthetic lace and had applied for patents on the method of producing it. They also had raised money from some angel investors or venture capitalists to fund a startup. They were in the process of equipping and staffing a production facility in Newark, with offices across the river in New York.

Constance was mildly curious, but she was far from excited. She thought, "It seems like a long shot that this synthetic lace idea will mean anything to me. I'm trying to downsize, not get in deeper over my head. I know Jeremy will hit the roof if I take on anything new like this. I don't see how it would fit with my traditional lace shop and hand-sewing business. Problem is, I don't know where else to turn. I have no other exit plan, but I know something has to be done."

Later that same day, Jeremy was at his office, having seen his last patient at about 4:30 p.m. He was removing his white jacket, as his Physician's Assistant, Angie Tatum, came in. "Heading home, Doctor?" she smiled.

"Haven't decided yet. Angie. I'm sort of tired. I think I could use a glass of white wine. Would you join me?" Jeremy responded, as he reached behind himself to open a small office refrigerator to retrieve a bottle.

"Sounds good," said Angie, as Jeremy pulled out two glasses and began pouring. "It's been pretty busy around here today, but fortunately no serious emergencies. It's always good to have a pause at the end of the day and do something enjoyable - be human, instead of being a medical robot. I'm talking about me, of course, not you. You are always cool, and yet warm, with patients. You can be matter of fact with a smile and a warm look in your eyes, and the patients seem to take comfort, even when they've been distressed. I'm not sure what it takes to be a good Doctor, but you've got it!"

"I don't know, Angie. I do what I need to do. It's good to have you, always at hand, but never in the way, just perfect, anticipating what I need before I ask you," Jeremy said. "I don't always get that treatment at home. Connie is such a bundle of nerves, and she has gotten clingy and jealous. She suspects I'm involved with someone else, and you are the number one suspect. She found some lipstick on my shirt collar once. You've got to change your lipstick shade, or she will convict us. I've got to be frank with you and say I'm torn between trying to make my marriage work and starting over with you. I find myself being drawn closer to you day by day, but I've got two kids, I live in a mansion, I have a rich father-in-law, and the community thinks Connie and I are the ideal couple. All that is good for business, especially when you are a pediatrician. But Connie has changed. She says she loves me, but behind it all, she's married to her shop, and she compartmentalizes our time, and gives preference to that damned shop. She says she wants to get away from the shop, sell it or close it, but she can't bring herself to do that. I'm beginning to think the romance has gone out of our lives, and she will tolerate me and try to keep me around, but I think she also wants to hang onto the shop. I just don't see anything changing."

"Jeremy, you are such a joy to be around, even when we're working hard. I don't know how anyone could just tolerate you and try to hold onto you as some sort of trophy while the affections are somewhere else. I know you have tough decisions to make, but I would love to just try to make you happy. We've always been a good team," Angie said with a searching look in her eyes.

"Thanks, Angie. You have already made me happy. You are right, though, I have a lot to think over and evaluate. I need to be honest with you and make sure you know that I can't promise you anything. We might just have to put our intimate feelings behind us and make it all strictly professional at some point. I am not there yet, but it could come to that. Could you live with an 'either-or' outcome a little longer, as I try to sort things out?" Jeremy asked.

"It won't be easy, but the answer is 'yes.' I can live with it day-by-day, and I can take the consequences, whatever they may be, because I love you. I'm strong for right now, Jeremy, but I don't know for how long," Angie replied.

"Well, this has been good and reassuring. I'd like to take you out to some nice restaurant that's way over on the other side of town, where no one knows either of us, but we have to be careful. Maybe another time. I think I'd better go home for now. I have a lot of thinking to do," Jeremy announced as he rose to leave.

"Then go, be strong, and know that I love you. Bye," said Angie. Jeremy nodded, gave her a hug, and they parted for the evening.

CHAPTER SEVENTEEN: A Conversation with Ted Born

Constance came into Ted Born's office, and Ted greeted her as she sat down. "Ted, I'm here because I have a decision to make, and I need your advice. This is not a legal question, at least not yet, but lawyers are called counselors, aren't they? And I trust your counsel."

"Connie, I get all kinds of questions people ask me. Sometimes I don't even ask myself whether it's a legal question. The truth is, almost everything we do has legal ramifications, and it's part of our job as lawyers to steer our clients away from future legal problems that don't exist yet. Sometimes we get questions where we have to say, 'that's out of my field,' or 'you need a shrink instead of a lawyer.' But, what's on your mind? I'll help if I can," Born said.

"Well, I have a decision to make, and I've thought about it so much I've just about worn out of patience with myself, going over and over it in my own mind," Constance began. "I need help. Okay, here's what it is. I let my guard down a little with one of my friends, a customer, about my frustration in trying to find a way to build enough value in my company to make it salable - because it sure isn't salable the way it is now. The friend happened to mention she had heard of a new company that had developed a kind of synthetic lace that you could sew on or iron onto other fabrics. It was just a casual comment. And I didn't take it seriously because I want to downsize, not take on another product and another set of problems. But I find myself at this dead end, and I managed to get a telephone number, and I called one of the principals in this startup business called 'Sim Lace' - stands for 'simulated lace.' I have to say, the conversation got my interest up. It surprised me that he was willing to talk with me in any depth, but he seemed as curious about what I am doing as I was about his process."

"I guess it never hurts to check all the boxes," observed Ted. "What did you find out?"

"These people have come up with a way to make relatively inexpensive polyester lace, so they say. It's never going to be an esthetic rival to fine needle lace or bobbin lace that we try to stock in our shop, but a lot of lace doesn't need to be of heirloom quality. Sometimes people just like something that gives a soft impression of fine lace, and there haven't been really good alternatives in the past, at least not in commercial quantities for general applications. You know, lace is different from embroidery because embroidery is stitched into an underlying fabric, while lace is a standalone product. Lace has open loops held together by a network of strands, something like a spiderweb. Sometimes a grid is used and the stitching sort of fills in the grid with designs that have enough open spaces to give it an airy appearance. Sometimes, innovative designers using traditional technology start with a piece of fabric and snip out much of the fabric to leave a lot of openness, but as far as I know they can't match the results of using threads only, with no cutting necessary," Constance explained.

"Okay, Connie. Thanks for the professorial-type explanation of lace making, but go on and tell me what this new process is," Ted prompted.

"Of course, he did not provide any details of his process - actually, I think there are several developers/investors involved. But he did tell me they had found a way to take a certain formulated type of polyester sheets and stamp out designs that are pretty intricate. They have to heat the sheets, but not too much, and the polyester is designed to resist melting, but it softens just enough to enable the stamping out to work. They then run the product through a chemical bath that eats away the rough edges of the product, resulting in something that looks like lace to a casual viewer who doesn't inspect it close-up. He says they are still working on getting the polyester to accept coloration - changing a stark white to an ecru or cream or some other shade. Obviously, the process is a lot cheaper than making lace the traditional ways, although it's probably never going to replace traditional lace for use on fancy clothes. He thinks this lace would work fine on curtains and draperies and furniture fabric where it would provide an elegant look that is not too costly. He thinks this will broaden the market in ways we haven't even thought of yet," Constance related.

"It's interesting, but, even if there is a potential market out there, it might be less than he thinks, because the trend seems to be to simplify things and get away from the fancy stuff. And, of course, every new market has to be nurtured and developed, which could take time and considerable money," Ted cautioned.

"Yes, but there is one thing I haven't mentioned yet," Constance responded knowingly. "They say they have developed an adhesive edge that they can integrate into their sim lace if desired. They can make simulated lace strips with a heat-sensitive edge along one of the flowing edges, and you can just take a hot iron, and iron it on to the backside edge of fabric you want to attach it to. Since the adhesive is on the backside of the main fabric, once the lace has been ironed on, the adhesive part is not visible when the fabric, with attached lace, is viewed from the front. Obviously, the commercial advantage is that the lace is easy to attach and can save hours of sewing. So, for those who aren't picky about great quality heirloom lace but like the general impression of lace, they can buy this sim lace and can apply it to all kinds of products, other than fancy children's clothes. It might be that my main problem at my shop, and its concept, is that people these days don't have the time, or don't want to take the time to make the effort to use the highest quality lace for limited projects. Maybe, it's not a matter of lace having lost its appeal; it's possible my marketing problem is that customers would be delighted to use more lace if it were easier to use. My guess is that they will settle for lower quality if it is easy to apply and looks all right when not subjected to a lot of scrutiny - probably the case with most people. After all, who comes into your home and starts inspecting the construction of your curtains and furniture fabric? The truth is: nobody."

Ted scratched his head and frowned slightly. "Connie, I think I'm following what you are saying, but how does that help you? Suppose all that they tell you is true and that they succeed in creating a vast new market for sim lace. It would certainly seem to hurt your already ailing business to some extent, maybe fatally. And if you start buying their sim lace and selling it yourself, how do you promote the sim lace and at the same time convince customers to buy your higher quality traditional lace? Aren't you likely to end up with an unfocused business with two different products that clash with each other, and you just have a glorious mess?"

"You have a point there, Ted, and I have been thinking about it," said Constance. "But there is one more angle that could have potential. The sim lace people, who are all men, need a knowledgeable female promoter or spokesperson to help put their product on the map, and when I told them about myself and background with lace, they said they would like to interview me for that possible slot. It could lead to an arrangement where the profit for being spokesperson would swallow up my lace boutique, and I could maybe use this opportunity, if it materializes, to convert my shop to a sideline location for the sim lace people, mainly for PR purposes, but I could still maintain it as my shop and office."

Ted still looked puzzled and had a slight frown on his face. "Connie, how is Jeremy going to react to this? Doesn't he want you to get out instead of getting in deeper? And how are you going to handle your children's needs at their young ages, assuming the sim lace people give you an opportunity to work with them in some way?"

"You hit the nail on the head. Jeremy's a potential roadblock. I haven't told him yet, as it seems premature to get him riled up over something that might never happen. As for the children, I don't know that there would be much travel involved; to take me away from them for any extended time. Maybe there would be, but that hasn't been discussed. It's possible that not much would change in my relationship with the children. But I do love them so, so much. Right now, I just want to explore this option. It might be a solution to my problems, or it might escalate the problems, but I will never know if I don't look into it further, right now, while this is still a hot new idea and the guys in New York seem interested. What do you think?" Constance asked.

"So, how do you plan to look into it further? What's next?" asked Ted.

"I need to go to New York and meet with these people and get them to explain it to me better and find out their ideas about how I could fit into the picture. They've told me they are willing to meet with me, so I just need to set a date and clear it with them. And when I go, Ted, I need you to go with me. I have to show them I have good counsel and will be getting good advice in evaluating any deal we might make, and I will need you to go with me. I hope you will do it. As a young woman from the South, I won't have any credibility; they'll try to run all over me Can you check your calendar and let me know what works for you? Then I can call them back and firm up a date," Constance implored.

"Well, yes, I can do that, Connie. I fly for corporate clients all the time. But I have to tell you about the expense. I will need my out-of-pocket expenses covered - airline ticket, hotel, and meals - and, unfortunately, I have to charge something for my travel time.

I will try to work on some matters for other clients while we have some 'dead' time at airports and on the airplane, when we aren't conferring about your strategy for the trip, so as to avoid charging you for all the time while I am away. You might have heard the old saying: 'a lawyer's time and advice is his stock-in-trade,' and, because I would be limited in what I can do for other clients while we are away, I have to charge something. However, at a maximum, I would charge for only six hours a day, although I almost always put in longer time than that in a typical day's work, and maybe I can charge less if I can do work for some other clients while we are en route. I warn you of this, Connie, because I know you are losing money at the shop, and I know you are having to watch pennies to keep going," Ted answered.

"Ted, I see this as a critical trip, and I understand what you are saying, but it's something I feel I have to do. I appreciate your being up-front with me, but I know you will be fair, and that's all I can expect. Okay. Can you give me some dates?" Constance asked.

Ted gave Constance several dates, knowing this trip would probably take at least two and possibly three days, including the travel time. Constance thanked him and said she would be back in touch soon. Ted thought to himself, "I've done a lot of traveling for clients, but rarely with an attractive young woman who is having domestic problems and business financial problems and seems somewhat desperate. I just have to remind myself, 'she's just like any other client - just be professional'."

CHAPTER EIGHTEEN:
The Dinner

Constance made the arrangements, booked and paid for the flight tickets, reserved two rooms at the Carlyle Hotel in New York, and she and Ted Born were on their way to an appointment with the Sim Lace founders. Ted did some research and found that Sim Lace - the actual name the company adopted - was essentially a start-up operation, but apparently a fairly well-funded startup. One or two patents had been granted and several more were pending on their simulated lace concepts. Constance and Ted decided they would check out the processes, to the extent possible, and ask enough questions to determine whether there might be a way for Constance to benefit from some sort of participation in the new product and technology. There was to be an exploratory and open-ended meeting. As promised, Ted tried to work on other legal matters while en route, to reduce Constance's expenses, making for a quiet flight with little conversation. The meeting would take place the day following their arrival, so they checked in the hotel, freshened up in their rooms, and took a table in the hotel restaurant.

After ordering drinks, Constance looked at Ted and said, "Ted, it just struck me that we have been working together now for more than a year, and you know a lot more about me than I know about you. You are always asking the questions - for me to answer. You know about me, my father, my husband, my legal and financial issues, even some of my marital problems, but all I know about you is that you are a fine lawyer."

"I suppose that's because I don't want to bill you for small talk. You come to me for professional advice or professional actions, and I try to restrict myself to dealing with your legal matters without interjecting myself into them. I am just trying to be 'your humble servant,'" Ted grinned. "But I told you I would not charge you for the time spent at after-hours meals, or overnight time, so I'm willing to answer your questions now, without charge, so if you have any, fire away."

"I'm not trying to pry, Ted, but I like to feel I know the person that I have come to depend on for so many things that are at the top of my list of serious challenges and on whom I am in some ways staking my future. I know you on one level, as a darn good lawyer, but that is not the same as knowing you as a person, what makes you tick. So, tell me, Ted, who are you?"

Ted laughed. "You might say that I, like everyone else, am a work in progress. I am still trying to discover who I am, day after day. Think of me as a piece of paper, where some things have been written and a lot else is yet to be written, and I am acutely aware of what the hand with the pencil is writing, as the story of my life unfolds. I know I cannot unwrite whatever is written, as I don't have a magic eraser. My only hope is in whatever comes next, and I have found it is a lot easier to make a mess of things than to get it right. And, to get it 'right,' I have to know what is right or at least make the best judgment I can."

"All right, said Constance, "let's start with what has already been written. Tell me about that, if you can do it without re-opening things that you feel are far too personal or too painful. I think your past will give a good hint as to what is yet to come."

Ted thought a moment, took a sip of his white wine, and said, "There's nothing special to tell, Connie. I am just an ordinary person. I don't have any remarkable pedigree. I certainly never had any money when I was growing up. I have worked hard all my life, starting when I was ten years old. I know, the Child Labor Laws technically would not have allowed me to work anywhere until, I think, when I became twelve, but I did it anyway - 40 cents an hour at first, and then, as I was given more hours to work, my pay was actually cut to 25 cents per hour. But I wouldn't take anything for the experience. I was working at a recreation center, checking out game equipment, selling soft drinks and candy, keeping the place clean and dealing with customers. I learned so much!"

"Makes me wonder if I'm not being overcharged with your fees today!" Constance teased. "What was your homelife like?"

"It was really great, looking back at it. We had chickens and a milk cow in our backyard, and even a Shetland pony that I loved to ride. We lived only a few blocks from downtown, but it was not unusual for people at that time to have farm animals in their backyard. Two of the other families on the same street also had chickens and cows, but no Shetland ponies! I was the caboose in my family, the youngest of six, one of whom had died young, so I had four older brothers and sisters, whom I tagged along behind and who took care of me a lot of the time, giving my parents some relief. We struggled financially, but I never felt deprived. Daddy worked terribly hard, at two different jobs. Our house was modest, but it all worked. To me, it never felt like we were on the lower rungs of the financial ladder, at least not until I became a teenager in high school, when my classmates were talking about college, and I didn't know where or whether I could go," Ted reminisced.

"But, as I recall, you did go to some fine colleges. How did you manage that?" Constance asked.

"Well, yes, it was almost accidental. I had a good record in high school - salutatorian of my graduating class, honor society, editor of the school newspaper, and lots of other recognitions. But I made no college plans until my senior year in high school;

actually, it was rare for high schoolers at that time to do much about college before their senior year. I'll spare you the details, but I got a scholarship to Columbia. I knew it was an Ivy League school, but what I didn't know was that, although I was an engineering major, I was required to take classes on the Great Books, the great philosophers, art humanities, music humanities, and I even wedged in courses on Oriental Civilization. Those courses changed my life; I never knew anyone ever had tried so hard to understand what life and culture was all about, until I read the writings of the great philosophers. And I would never have taken those courses if they had not been mandatory. A magnificent accident! But excuse me, I'm talking too much, got carried away, and I've been telling you a lot more than you want to know," Ted said apologetically.

"No, Ted, for the first time I think I am getting acquainted with the real Ted Born. But one more thing: How did an engineering student end up in law school? Didn't you go to the University of Virginia?" Constance asked.

"Yes, I went to UVA Law School - again, a sort of an accident. I went to college intending to be a pre-law student, not knowing much about the law but having been captivated by legal mystery writers like Erle Stanley Gardner. However, I had this feeling that science and technology would be increasingly important in the future, and my faculty adviser was wise enough to tell me that these were not diametrically opposed interests, that a scientific major was as good as, if not better than, anything else as preparation for a legal career. So, I went the engineering route but never took my eye off the law. Somehow, Virginia gave me a scholarship, and I arrived there, not really knowing what to expect and wondering what I had gotten myself into. But I have hardly ever been happier than at Virginia, and it translated into a good academic record. So, now, you know the story of my background, and I think the waiter is getting impatient about our placing orders for dinner!" Ted concluded.

"Okay, let's go ahead and order. I know you have had a great legal career and family life, but that can wait," Constance said, as she scanned the menu under the patient presence of the waiter.

It took a while for dinner to arrive. Afterward, it was getting late, and tomorrow would be a full day. They rose from the table and started to the elevator to go to their adjacent rooms. Ted wondered to himself if he should give her a hug before retiring but thought better of it, counseling himself silently, "This has been a highly personal evening where I have bared my soul to her, and she was obviously interested. I know she is having marital problems, and this evening could very well take a highly unprofessional turn. He thought of Lydia, back in Greenville. I can't let that happen. I should shake hands with her, like I would do with any other client, and bid her a good and restful night." He did that, and he thought he detected a hesitant and, maybe, disappointed look on her face. But he knew he could not be effective as her lawyer and at the same time be a part of a triangle with Constance and Jeremy. It would be unprofessional, and it would be wrong. They said their "Good Nights," and went into their separate rooms.

CHAPTER NINETEEN:
Sim Lace

Sim Lace had its office in Midtown, not so far from the Carlyle, but Constance opted for a taxi. They arrived at the Sim Lace offices, took the elevator up to the 14th Floor. It was not impressively furnished, but neither Ted nor Constance had expected anything fancy except, perhaps, the simulated lace itself. The receptionist left her desk to take them to a conference room, where they were offered coffee and tea. Shortly, the receptionist ushered in Maurice LaFere and Vincent Bocelli, who introduced themselves as co-CEOs of Sim Lace.

Vincent began, "Let us tell you a little bit about ourselves. Maurice - I've always called him Maury - and I are products of the Garment District, around West 35th Street, not far from Macy's. Our mothers were both seamstresses there, mine from Italy and Maury's from France, and by coincidence we grew up as friends and neighbors in the westside tenements. Both of our mothers, though, were upscale seamstresses, making wedding dresses and fancy clothes, and both of them loved lace. You know, there was a strong Italian tradition with lace, and likewise a strong tradition in France, that later spread over into Belgium, a country that became famous for its lace. I grew up, got an MBA, and went to work as a stockbroker. Maury opened up a high-class dress shop which is patronized by some of New York's finest. But we remained friends, and both of us have inherited our mothers' love of beautiful laces. Unfortunately, we both regretted that beautiful laces have been going out of style, partly because the finest of them are getting scarcer, and the general public is not exposed to them much today."

Maurice interjected, "The handmade lace has become almost nonexistent, and the bobbin lace is also fading out. It is just too labor intensive to make, and the public sees very little of it, mainly on some wedding dresses and veils, or in old photographs and paintings. People rarely think of it in other contexts. Vinnie and I got to thinking, what if we could find a way to make lace go mainstream.? How could we make it more plentiful and lower its cost, not only to make, but to use on clothing and other fabrics after it is made? How could we do that? Well, Vinnie has contacts in the world of high finance, and I have contacts in the dressmaking industry, so, we decided to see what we could do. To make a long story short - and it is a long story - we found some people who could stamp out designs on pieces of polyester fabric. What they were doing at that time wasn't very refined, but we wondered if it could be improved and adapted to be able to make low-cost lace that would be acceptable for a lot of applications in the mass market, with the hope that, over time, the quality could get better and better, and acceptable applications would develop. Now, let me be frank about it. We never expected to be able to make a product that anywhere near rivaled fine handmade lace, but we were hopeful to make a product that would be suitable for less demanding usages, with hopes for incremental improvement from time to time. It was a tough assignment."

Vincent stepped back in. "I accidentally ran across a company in my study of initial public offerings of stock, that could stamp out designs in polyester fabric. They were not working with anything like lace, but it occurred to Maury and me that a refined version of the process might be adaptable to making lace. What we developed was very promising, and some of the process is proprietary, and we cannot share it with you, but I can tell you that we take photographs of genuine pieces of fine lace, and by a delicate and complicated process the photograph is used to produce an engraved image that can be used to stamp out simulated lace. Here are some samples we've made by this process."

Vincent laid the samples on the desk in front of Constance and Ted. Maurice cautioned, "Now, even though these are fantastic results from what we were getting in the beginning, we realize that no one would mistake this product for genuine fine handmade lace. But we think there is a market for it, and as our process is improved, the market should expand. There are some rough edges in places on our synthetic lace, but we can get rid of most of them by running our raw output through a chemical bath that dissolves or eats away the spurious bits and pieces along the edges without destroying the main tendrils of the lace. In fact, the chemical bath has a beneficial effect on the sim lace by softening it, without weakening it materially, and giving it more of a true lace look and texture."

Maurice volunteered, "There are three big hurdles that have to be overcome. First you must have a type of polyester fabric strong enough to withstand the stamping process, and ours has been specially developed to do that. Second, you have to have a stamp impression that is fine enough and sharp enough to cut a pattern out of the polyester without chopping it up and making a big mess. Finally, you have to be able to eliminate all or most of the rough imperfections in the impressed sim lace so as to make it commercially acceptable to those who want a low-price simulated lace, where a casual look gives a basic impression of lace that does not have to meet rigid standards. We feel good about our progress and expect even greater improvements along the way. Now that you know something about us and our products, I would like to hear your story of where you are, and whether you think you might be able to fit into our future plans, or vice versa."

Constance responded, "I can see that you have a very interesting process and at least the beginnings of a simulated lace that could suit certain applications. My situation is that I got interested in delicate hand sewing of clothes for my small children, where lace can be a critical factor in the end product. I got so fascinated with it that I opened a shop, originally with a partner, who is no longer with me. The shop has a devoted clientele, but not yet enough patronage to make it profitable in the foreseeable future. My interest in your product is to see if it could provide enough volume for my store to enable my store to turn a profit. It's intriguing, but I don't know whether your product is a good fit with my store, which really is a kind of purist enclave. My husband, a pediatrician, is doubtful that I can ever make a success of my shop. Mr. Born is my attorney, who has seen me through some difficult situations, and I also lean on him for business advice, which is why he is here."

Maurice spoke up. "We did a little checking on you before you came, and we found out that you do have an upscale shop with upscale clientele. And we found that you and your husband are fixtures in the South Carolina social scene. It's obvious that you are bright and well-spoken, and - if you don't mind my saying so - you are very attractive. You make a very good appearance. We anticipate that the South could be one of our prime targets for growth because of its cultural background, in fine and fashionable clothing and home interiors. I gather Charleston is well known for culture and good taste. Now you are not technically from Charleston, but I would guess Greenville is close enough. I haven't talked with Vinnie about it, but I can see some potential in your becoming a spokesperson for our product, and your shop could be one of the epicenters of our promotional efforts. Is that a concept you think we could explore further?"

"Well, you take me by surprise, as I was focusing just on my shop, and I don't quite know what to say. I am just exploring possibilities at this point. We would have to get more specific, maybe do a test run to see if it could work," Constance said, looking at Ted. "You see, I am also a mother of two young children, and I am already stretched pretty thin. Could you be more specific?"

Vinnie responded, "we would have to think it out, too. It is an evolving concept, and we, like you, are not at all sure it would work. But here's my thinking. Maury and I are businesspeople. We have been tinkering with the technical production issues and we can foresee that we can produce a product that should be marketable. But there's a cultural angle involved in the marketing, and Maury and I know we are not the ones whose faces will promote the product. Somehow, we need a spokesperson who is culturally credible to be the face of our product - appearing in ads, TV commercials, doing some demonstrations, that kind of thing. You might or might not be the right person for us, but I think it might be worth checking out."

"What do you have in mind that I would actually do?" Constance asked.

"We don't have details worked out, but it would include TV spots where you would showcase our lace and promote it, with some of the shots taken at your boutique. There would be some print ads as well in selected fashion magazines, curtain and furniture manufacturer ads, and maybe in Junior League and other young women's publications. Maybe we could warehouse some of the product in Greenville, and you could help with fulfillment orders. There might be some in-person demonstrations and lectures involved. You could end up as something of a celebrity. We of course would pay you for your services and out-of-pocket expenses. A big benefit to you would be helping you develop a mail-order business for your handmade lace that could piggy-back on our business," Maurice ventured.

"Hmm," Constance mused. "This is not at all what I was thinking when I came here, but maybe it makes sense. I've done a little acting in high school and college productions, but nothing beyond that. We could shoot a trial TV shot, and take a look at it and see if I would project the impression you are looking for, and that would give us all an idea whether this is a project that could be developed further. What do you think, Ted?"

"I can see some potential in the ideas we are batting around, but of course the details make all the difference. How would Constance be compensated?" Ted asked.

"We are thinking, maybe, $500 per spot, plus out-of-pocket expenses. You have to realize that we are a startup and have all kinds of heavy expenses before any income is realized. I know it is not a lot of money, but, if it works, Constance might gain celebrity status that would be worth quite a lot of money to her and her business. Print ads would be more like $100 per ad, and we would have the right to re-use indefinitely without additional compensation. Want to give it a try?" Maurice said.

"We have to realize that Constance would be taking a risk because she is not just an actress or a model, but a store owner with an upscale clientele, and the last thing she would want is for her customers to think she has changed over from fine handmade lace and is offering nothing but sim lace. She is here because she wants ideas that would help her make her existing business more profitable, and she will need to be very careful to 'do no harm' to her existing business while participating in some way with you. Constance and I need to talk privately and try to figure whether there is a way to make this work, a way that makes sense both for you and for Constance. While I can see potential opportunity here, it is something that needs to be thought out carefully. I would assume that, if Constance tried to sell your product alongside her present lines, you would give her a discount, on presumably a most-favored-nations basis. This would give her an incentive to try to push your product through her store at the same time she is selling her handmade lace. Maybe Constance and I could take a short break and then reconvene with you in, say, half an hour. Is there a room we can use?"

Ted and Constance were shown to another room. Ted said, "Connie, I don't want to be so conservative that I cause you to miss an opportunity to solve the pressing problem you are facing right now in your Greenville store. However, before you jump into this new frying pan, I want to be sure you have considered all the angles. In the first place, you are very busy right now with your store responsibilities and your home responsibilities, and you are considering piling more responsibilities on top of the considerable ones you already have. I realize that, if your deal with these Sim Lace people is a great success, it could solve your present problems with your boutique. But you also don't want to get into a new set of responsibilities without having a way out if it isn't working well for you. So, you need an exit strategy. You also need to get very specific about your duties and responsibilities to Sim Lace, and be sure you are fairly compensated for your work. I guess the first thing you need to do is to have a trial run at doing a TV commercial for them. If it looks good, it will give you some leverage negotiating your deal. If it doesn't go well, then you are likely back at Square One, but at least you haven't entangled yourself in a program that doesn't do any good for anybody. My thought is that we do a test run at creating a TV ad and go on from there."

"Sounds good, Ted. But they will have to give me the script and educate me about the product, so I can do a convincing job. Let's go back and resume our meeting," Constance concurred.

At the meeting, all agreed that a trial run at a TV ad would be the first step, and it so happened that the Sim Lace officials had a draft script in hand, prepared by an ad agency. "This probably needs some editing and polishing," said Vinnie, "but it might be a good enough first cut to be useful for our present purposes." Maurice and Vincent then handed the synthetic lace to Constance and positioned her in front of a pre-prepared backdrop and brought in the camera. Constance went through the script without the camera a few times, and then they took some reel footage on the camera. When they played it back, it looked good. Constance exuded Southern charm and poise as she made the pitch, and it was clear from the reactions of the two officials that they had just discovered the star they had been hoping to find.

Vinnie spoke first, "If you can do this good without any real preparation or tutoring, you ought to be great in a real commercial take. I think we would like to see if we can work with you. We'll come down to Greenville as well, and we should be able to see better just how we can structure our relationship."

"Okay," said Constance. "I kind of enjoyed that. Let's see if we can work it out."

"We'll be in touch," Vinnie assured her, as they shook hands, and the meeting broke up.

CHAPTER TWENTY:
The Assessment

The plane ride back to Greenville, with a short layover in Atlanta, gave Constance and Ted a chance to talk about what had just happened in New York. At first there were some congratulations from Ted to Constance, and then there was a period of quiet, broken when Constance said, "Ted, I don't really know what I have accomplished and whether it makes sense for me, and I don't even have a proposal from Vinnie and Maurice. What do I do next? And how does it solve the problems I already have?"

"Good questions, Connie," Ted responded. "I've been sitting here asking myself the same questions. My answer has been, 'Let's not get ahead of ourselves. Let's see what they propose, and then we face the questions you just raised.' I look at it this way: Before the trip to New York, there didn't seem to be any good avenues for coping with your problems. Now there is, possibly, a positive development. Now there is hope. It might not work, but at least it is something. You are going to have to think it through when you get the proposal."

Connie frowned and said, "I don't know what I say to my present customers who have been hearing me tout the virtues of fine hand sewing, and now I have to go on TV and tell the world how great this synthetic lace is. How do I handle that?"

Ted had a possible answer. "You know, Connie, that there are car dealerships that sell top-of-the-line cars and also middle level cars. They just tell their customers that they carry a range of models that all have their place, depending on your needs and what suits you, and help the customers settle on something. Isn't that logical?"

"Maybe, and I guess it helps that our traditional fine lace has an almost entirely different application from simulated lace," Constance said thoughtfully. "The traditional is for delicate and fancy clothing, and the sim is mainly for curtains and furniture. Still, there might be a dilution effect. I have really been promoting traditional lace as the ultimate in fashion, with nothing to compare. Now, I will have to say there is a place for synthetic lace as well. Of course, any person with any knowledge of lace will readily know the difference, but would there be less knowledgeable potential customers who might wonder if our shop would be passing off the synthetic for the traditional? We are trying to broaden the market for fine lace. Will we be turning some people off if we take on the promotion of simulated lace? I don't know."

"I don't know either," Ted responded. "I only know that those potential customers you are concerned about are not showing up much in your patronage bottom line. The rate of new 'conversions' to the cult worship of traditional lace seems to be very modest, and you need to broaden your appeal, so maybe the simulated product opens up a bigger market faster than your focus on traditional lace. I'm a lawyer, not a merchant, but it seems to me you almost have to think in terms of doing something different if your shop is to survive, or if it is to survive long enough so that it can be off-loaded on an acceptable basis - which I understand is your main goal. How do you think Jeremy is going to react to this development?"

"Jeremy is not going to like it. He might even be adamantly opposed. But, if I go through with the Sim Lace option, I will be doing it largely for the sake of my family, and with the thought of eventually getting an albatross off my neck. I don't know of any other options," Constance thoughtfully responded.

Indeed, when Constance arrived back at Helicon Heights in Greenville, Jeremy blew up, saying, "Connie, what a stupid thing to even consider! You are supposed to be shedding the shop, not complicating it and our lives more. You have failed with traditional fine lace, and now you think the solution is to extend yourself further - and into a market you know nothing about. I know you don't want to face your father with your failure, but it's something you have to do. Hanging on out of false pride and fear of embarrassment is not the answer. Your father will survive the loss. Just face up to it and be done with it!"

"Look, Jeremy," Constance began. "I knew you would feel this way, but hear me out for a couple of minutes. First, I want to put this 'lace phase' of my life behind me as much as you do, maybe more. And, if I undertake this Sim Lace project, I would only do it if I were convinced it would bring me closer to that goal. I am looking on this possible project as a fairly brief interim deal to add quick value and appeal to my shop so I can sell it for a reasonable price. It would be premature to make a judgment until we see the proposal of the Sim Lace people. We should get the proposal within a few days and then we can decide. Let's not burn any bridges behind us, or any bridges to the future."

Jeremy was silent for a moment, and then he said, "I've told you what I think, and you know how I feel. Now I leave it to you. The consequences are in your hands. I'm going to bed - alone." He stalked out of the room.

The children were already in bed. Constance went to the kitchen cabinet, opened a bottle, and shook out two pills, poured some water into a paper cup and swallowed them. Then she sat on a sofa in the downstairs den, turned on the television and sat numbly, unconscious of what was on the screen. "Why do I feel so trapped and so alone? There may be larger problems impinging on the world and its geopolitics, but this one looms heavy over my head, and I don't know what to do. What do I do? Where do I turn? I want to fly like an eagle, make something of my life, and I'm stranded here on this firmament, which is not feeling all that firm right now."

CHAPTER TWENTY-ONE: The Decision

Back in New York, Maurice LaFere and Vincent Bocelli were talking in the Sim Lace offices. Maurice said, "First thing we have to decide is, do we like this lady Constance, and can we work with her? She's a society girl, her dad's a professor, and her husband is a pediatrician. She made a pretty good appearance on that one trial TV take, and she's from the South where we think we might develop a good market. But how exactly do we use her in our program, and what's it gonna cost us? We are a start-up, and we are burning through money, and not much is coming in."

"The one thing I see is for her to make some TV ads for us and maybe some print ads," Vincent offered. "Our products are lightweight and easy to ship, so we don't need her shop to serve as a warehouse for our lace, other than having some good displays on hand. If our market develops well, and if we think her 'starring' in the commercials is the reason, we might want her to go on some promotional goodwill trips to speak to some women's groups. She's pushing her own fine lace right now, but that's a limited local market, and I don't see that as a conflict of interest. In fact, it might help if she goes on the air and says something like, 'I know fine traditional lace and appreciate it, but now that I've discovered Sim Lace, I'm amazed at how beautiful it is.' I tend to agree with you that there's potential for her to do us some good, if we can figure it out, and if we can afford her. However, we've got to make it worth her while, without breaking the bank.

"Looks like what we need to do is to nail her down with an annual retainer that she gets regardless of what we ask her to do, and then pay her for individual assignments. Do you think she might agree to a $10,000 annual retainer, plus $1000 for each TV spot she does, plus out-of-pocket expenses? And if we ask her to do anything else, like TV/radio celebrity interviews, we could negotiate the compensation. This would be like found money to her, supplementing her shop income. How about that?" Vincent continued.

Maurice nodded his head. "Yeah, we need to give her enough to keep her happy, and it could turn out to be one of our best investments. Let's try that and see if it flies."

Vincent was nominated to make the call to Constance. "Hi, Constance, this is Vinnie in New York. Maury and I enjoyed meeting with you and your lawyer. Hope all is well with you in Greenville."

"We're fine in Greenville, just trying to build a business and a clientele - a lot of work, but it's fun," Constance fudged a bit.

"That's good," said Vincent. "You know, Maury and I like you, and we like your style. We have a pathway that we've come up with that we think would make us all winners, you and us. We would like you to be on board with us on a kind of 'as-needed' basis. We would pay you a retainer of $10,000 a year, payable monthly, but it's firm and you would get it regardless of how much or how little we called on you to do. In addition to that, we would pay you a flat fee of $1000 for each TV spot we called on you to do for us. We of course would own all rights to the slots and could run them as often or as infrequently as we saw fit. We would be feeling around for other projects, like TV or radio celebrity interviews, and we would just negotiate the price for that. We just aren't sure what might come up and how we might need you, but we would work with you one-at-a-time on those projects. Of course, we would reimburse you for all out-of-pocket expenses. We think this is a good deal for you because you have the possibility of achieving celebrity status which would benefit your shop and your career in many ways, and, in the meantime, it would help pay the overhead. What do you think?"

Constance was guarded in her response. "Thank you for calling, Vinnie. I'll need a little time to think this over, discuss it with my lawyer, Ted Born, and of course my family. At a minimum, I would need advance notice of these sessions for TV spots as well as other projects and would have to consider the costs of making backup arrangements for my shop, and there would be a cost for me in hiring backup arrangements for my children while I was working with you. Do you anticipate there would be much traveling involved that would take me out of town?"

"Of course, you can talk it over with your lawyer and family. We don't expect an on-the-spot answer. But we are busy making our plans, and we presume you are also, so let's try to sort things out and resume our discussions. And if you have innovative ideas of how you could fit in with our business, we would like to hear them. We're in the learning process and are in the market for any ideas you might have. Let's plan to get back together on the phone sometime in the next week or so. Good talking with you, and say hello to Ted and your husband."

"Will do. Thanks for calling, Vinnie. Bye."

Constance immediately called Ted Born and arranged to come by his office and see him after the shop closed. When she got there and was ushered into Ted's office by his secretary, who was about to leave for the day, Constance said, "Ted, I need advice - real bad!" Constance related the telephone call from Vincent Bocelli. "I don't know what to do, Ted. The retainer is a good thing, and they have doubled the $500 figure they mentioned in New York as a payment for each TV spot; now the amount is $1000. My dilemma is that all of this helps somewhat, but it doesn't solve my basic problem. That is, it binds me to this shop and to the lace business when I need to get out, for financial, personal, and marital reasons. The lease on the shop costs me $36,000 per year, and I have employees to pay, and also a nanny to pay who would otherwise be unnecessary. I have all kinds of other expenses, like advertising, telephone and other utilities, inventory, and every charity in town expects me to make contributions. While $10,000 a year helps, I would still be going in the hole every day I keep my doors open. I don't know how much income I would get from the TV spots; if I'm lucky, I would guess maybe $5000. So, I might get $15,000 a year out of it, in total. But my income from the sale of lace is very modest, a small market in the best of circumstances and a dying business after Kate walked out on me. Yes, I did get some money out of Kate in the lawsuit, and that has enabled me to keep the doors open as long as I have, but it can't go on forever like this. And I have a husband who seems to delight in my misery - no sympathy, no encouragement, no helpful advice. I am still caught in an insoluble dilemma. What do I do about it?"

Ted rubbed his chin, thought for a moment, and said, "I see only these options. First, you could try to negotiate a higher retainer from Sim Lace. I just don't know how high they might realistically go, because - although they like you - you are not yet a celebrity with a following, and they could probably hire people through a PR firm at a net cost cheaper than they have agreed to pay you. A second option would be to accept the proposed deal and hope that you would develop a celebrity status that would likely solve your problems with the shop and with Sim Lace. The third alternative would be to bankrupt the shop and forget about both the shop and Sim Lace."

"But I am a fighter, Ted, and a dreamer, too. I keep looking for a way to keep my dreams alive, my family intact, and to honor my father's confidence in me. Pride may run before the fall, and I might fail, but I have too much pride to go to Dad at this point and tell him what a mess I have made of things," Constance said with an air of determination, coupled with regret and remorse.

"Then," Ted advised, "it appears to me you should negotiate with Sim Lace as best you can, and then wow the public, nationally and locally, as a spokesperson for Sim Lace that will pull your shop through and create a celebrity persona of yourself that will open up all kinds of opportunities. That is a tall order and, I would venture, few people ever achieve it, unless there is a lot of luck to boot."

"I'm going to give it a try. That's what I'm going to do. I won't give up, at least, not yet," Connie announced. The meeting was over.

Constance was able to get the retainer up to $12,500 per year and the TV spots up to $1250. She confronted her husband Jeremy with her decision, without apologies and without pleading for his help, sympathy or understanding. The job now was to establish herself as some degree of a celebrity spokesperson for lace.

CHAPTER TWENTY-TWO: To Make it Work

Constance was the featured spokesperson for Sim Lace in two ad spots, one of which had run nationally and the other was held in readiness for release, depending on the success of the first one. She had begun to get compliments from acquaintances who had seen the spots. It was yet too early to determine whether the spot had produced a surge in the sale of Sim Lace's product. Important to Constance was whether the spot ad had affected the business of her shop, whether negatively or positively, and it was still too early to determine that, either. Constance was concerned that some of her clientele for traditional fine lace might think she had depreciated the value of her shop's main product by promoting a cheap synthetic lace. She had agreed to display and attempt to sell simulated lace at her shop, and she had gotten a number of curious inquiries about it but had not sold much.

"I know what I'll do," Constance said to herself. "I will write a book about lace, and I will deal with both types of lace and will clearly distinguish between the different applications for the traditional versus the synthetic lace. That way, I can clarify the roles of the different types of lace and hopefully help the market for both of them, and this should combat the damaging notion of some that I'm promoting two lace types that are inconsistent and competitive. It shouldn't be too hard. I will have lots of photographs, with some explanatory material about the photographs. It can be a short book that won't cost a lot but one that's easy to read and can lead to a better understanding of what I'm trying to do. I will either self-publish it or get a local publisher to take it on."

Constance decided she needed a manager for her business, freeing her to devote herself to creative promotional projects. She thought she knew the ideal person to take on the management responsibilities - Marcie Steinberg. Marcie was an enthusiast of delicate4 hand sewing, like Constance, and Constance had known her socially and through their mutual sewing circles for some years. Marcie had never been employed, because she did not need to be, as her family had money and a successful business. However, Marcie read the Wall Street Journal faithfully and was loosely involved in business decisions relating to her family business. "She is sharp as a tack, energetic, and knows a lot about lace," Constance told herself. "I think she'd be ideal if she will take it on."

Constance broached the subject with Marcie, and Marcie reluctantly agreed, but for $2000 per month, with flex time built in. "I'm not planning to spend eight hours a day at the shop, Constance, but I will make sure the bases are covered, that there are always qualified salespeople on the job, and that we handle the inventory and accounting properly," Marcie told Constance, who had hoped that her friendship with Marcie would enable her to get a better deal. Still, Marcie seemed the right person, and she needed a good manager, so Constance agreed.

Constance told Jeremy she had hired a manager for the business, and this should allow her to spend more time with the family. She thought Jeremy would respond positively to the manager development, because he was always complaining that the shop was so consuming for Constance that their home life had suffered badly. But Jeremy frowned when he heard how much Marcie would be paid and said, "Connie, where is the money going to come from? You are already paying $3000 a month rent, and you have maintenance, utilities, advertising expenses, inventory, legal expenses, and the shop is underperforming and doesn't seem to be getting any better. Connie, you can't afford Marcie!"

Connie stood her ground, "Jeremy, the business is about to take off. The national ads I'm doing for Sim Lace are going to do wonders. I'm on the road to being famous. Customers are soon going to come to the store in droves. We are right on the cusp of a tremendous breakthrough if we make the right decisions. And one of the right decisions is to get a good manager. I know I can't do everything, and I - we - have to have a home life. I don't think I have any choice, and Marcie is the right person."

Jeremy shook his head in dismay and said, "Connie, that store has always been a heavy weight you've been carrying. I hope you are right, but I am not at all sure that the national publicity you will be getting for the synthetic lace ads is going to translate into more sales and profits for your local store. You are always going to have to depend on local patronage, and people just are not going to become fine hand-sewing buffs because they saw you in a TV ad, and advertising a different product, too. I don't see any good coming out of it. As I see it, the albatross is about to crash and take you down with it."

"I've thought of that," said Constance. "I know that nothing is guaranteed in life. But sometimes you have to take risks. We may be in a tunnel now, but I think I see light at the end. Look, I'm writing this book about lace, explaining all about the different types of laces and what you can do with them. The local newspaper will cover me and my book, and my shop, and it is going to be a celebrity destination for shoppers. I'm making a big push to sell our kits, which can be shipped everywhere, with the right amount of lace in each one and with instructions for using the lace on different outfits. I just know it's going to be a big success. We just have to believe and try our darndest to make it happen. In the meantime, I will be released from day-to-day work so I can think and plan strategically."

"Well, while you are thinking and planning strategically, you might try adding up the expenses and compare them with the income," Jeremy replied pessimistically. "Not only are you running a deficit at the store, but you seem to have forgotten that we have expenses for our magnificent Greek-styled home on Helicon Heights. When we bought the house, we took out a mortgage, and we borrowed the down-payment from your dad. Then we had all those remodeling expenses to make it look more like a Greek temple. Your dad helped on those expenses also. You and I have split the repayments we've made so far, but you are not going to be able to contribute to future repayment because you are overloaded with debt and expenses for the shop. Your dad has been very generous, and I know you have told him we are not going to ask him for any more money. But I ask you, where is the money coming from to cover your shop expenses, pay off your share of the mortgage and loan repayments to your dad? Remember, we also have these nanny expenses, the private school expenses coming up for the children, and our normal household expenses. Where's it all coming from, Connie? As you know, I have a heavy student debt load from college and medical school, and my pediatrician's income can't be counted on to fill the gaps in our expenses. How do we make it work? Tell me!"

"I believe in what I'm doing. I have confidence. Somehow, I'll make it work. Just bear with me," Constance replied.

CHAPTER TWENTY-THREE: Some Months Later

Constance had finished her book, and she inquired whether Sim Lace would want to publish the book and distribute it through its national sales channels. "We'll take a look at it, Connie," Vinnie Bocelli told her. "We continue to be optimistic, but our sales are disappointing thus far. It has nothing to do with your ad spots. Every time we do a booster rerun of your ads, we get a bump in our sales, which tells us your ads have had a positive impact. Maybe your book would help. Send me a draft or mock-up to look over. Of course, I know in general how you were planning to lay out the book, and it seemed you were on the right course. Maybe that's a shot in the arm we need. How's your boutique doing?"

"It's hanging in there. I think our new manager is doing a good job, but I keep looking to turn the corner in a big way, and it just hasn't happened yet. We have a pretty good demand for our kits which we sell on-site and via mail, but there's a lot of expense measuring and including the right amount of lace in each kit, and the kits come in a number of patterns, and the amount of lace, and the colors, vary by pattern. And then we have to insert the correct pattern instructions with the proper kit. It's not as simple as it seems," Connie responded. "Anyway, I'll send you a draft of my book. It's essentially finished, but probably needs a little tweaking here and there."

Connie sent the book, and shortly got a call back from Vinnie. "Connie, we like your book. We might invest a little in getting the book into print. But the book is not going to promote itself. We need to do a TV spot showing you with your book, and then see if we can set you up for some appearances and book signings. That should create some buzz for your and our lace. There would be some expense involved, of course. We would pay for the ad spot as usual, and we would pay for half your expenses in doing the special appearance and book-signings. Of course, any profits from the sale of your books at these appearances would be yours. How does that sound?"

"Sounds reasonable," Connie agreed, glad to have someone pick up the expense of printing the book. "I just want to be sure the copyright is held solely in my name."

"No doubt about that. It's all yours. We are just looking on it as another marketing angle that could pay off. We think we won't be running the national ad spots for a while. It's so expensive to do that. We want to do more targeted marketing, like, to interior decorators. Your book would be something we could put in their hands that they could share with clients," Vinnie explained.

Constance thought it was about time to talk with Ted Born again. "Ted, I wanted to touch base with you and tell you where we are on my lace projects. First, you know that I have hired a manager who seems to be doing a good job. One of the bright spots at my shop is the sale of kits. But that turns out to be more complicated than I expected. One of the problems is in measuring the amount of lace to put in each kit, remembering that there are different amounts and colors of lace; it's not all white, some is ecru, some is blue, some pink. I have set up a table with two poles sticking up, exactly one yard apart. I have employees who measure out the lace by lapping the lace around the poles. It's crude and time consuming, but we haven't figured out a better way to do it. The bottom line, though, it that our total sales have been rather stagnant, despite the national TV ads that the Sim Lace folks are paying for, and despite some local advertising and some sewing classes we have put on. We are selling some of the sim-type lace, but most of those sales are going through the national company, and we don't share in any of those profits. Sim Lace has agreed to pay for publication of my lace book, and we will have that to put into peoples' hands, providing them with information and a reminder that we are still around and would like to sell something to them. By the way, I am not sure how well the national sales of Sim Lace are going. They don't give me any figures, but I am sensing they are disappointed and, like me, they are looking for a way to kick up the sales."

"So, what is your own profitability situation?" Ted asked.

"It's a problem, Ted," Connie confessed. "That's one of the main reasons why I wanted to talk with you. I'm losing money every month. I am burning through the money you won for us in the lawsuit with Kate Lord and, even though Sim Lace is paying me a little more than $1000 a month as a kind of consulting fee they call a retainer, and $1250 for each TV spot, we've only done two TV spots, and the pay I'm getting from Sim Lace won't even cover the cost of my manager. There's $3000 a month I have to pay in rent for the shop, and all kinds of other expenses. The lease for the shop still has about eighteen months to go, so I don't have an easy option to close down. I have to find a way to energize the sales far beyond what they are now, or . . ."

"Or bankruptcy?" Ted asked.

"Heavens, no! Bankruptcy is out of the question. It would be an incredible black spot and embarrassment both to my husband Jeremy and to my dad, and Jeremy would likely lose clients who wouldn't patronize a doctor with bad credit. Even more importantly, I could not live with myself. I would have let so many people down, and Jeremy would never let me hear the end of it, with all his scolding and 'I-told-you-so' attitude Jeremy is hard enough to live with as it is, and I have become very resentful of him and his smugness, seeming to enjoy seeing me struggle. No, bankruptcy is out of the question, at least for now."

"Well, there is an intermediate possibility," Ted counseled. "You might be able to cut a deal to settle with your creditors on a discount basis, gradually paying the agreed-upon compromise payments on a monthly pro-rata basis. You could do that quietly, without the publicity of bankruptcy, and would have the satisfaction of having made peace with everyone on an equitable and agreeable basis."

"I guess that might be better than bankruptcy, if I could work that out, but it still would not solve my problems with Jeremy, who would hold it over my head that I was a failure. My dad would also be disappointed in me, although he would be kind and diplomatic about it, which would hurt almost as badly as Jeremy's undisguised antagonism. Any other options?" Constance asked.

"Of course, you might try once again to sell the shop. It's been a while since you've tried, and there have been a lot of developments since that time, with all the publicity and the national relationship with the Sim Lace group. Somebody with a wad of money might want to take this on as a kind of hobby project and might be willing to assume all your debts. It's an upscale project and might appeal to someone's ego," Ted counseled. "You likely wouldn't make any profit out of it, but there are satisfactions in being the founder of a business that has continued on under new ownership. There's no shame in that. Of course, the purchaser would have to know that the business has not been profitable but would have enough money and confidence to take it on anyway, recognizing that many early startups have trouble making it at first and then turn the corner. Lots of restaurants are like that, a tough start, but then they make it."

"You are right. I haven't tried to sell the business in a while. Maybe I'll try that. The problem is, there is such a narrow band of people who know anything about lace or would otherwise have an interest, I can't imagine who would buy it," Constance mused.

"Get a good broker or real estate agent involved. They have contacts with a lot of people that you wouldn't even know about. It always surprises me that, when a business is put on the market, sometimes people come out of nowhere, that you would never expect. I think it is worth a try," Ted advised.

"You've encouraged me, Ted, given me some hope. I guess that's why they call you a counselor," Connie said gratefully. "I always feel better when I've talked with you."

"Well, my problem, Connie, is that I know precious little about lace, and most of what I know I have learned from you. So, I am a counselor who, in this case, starts with a disadvantage. But I hope things work out well for you."

CHAPTER TWENTY-FOUR: Constance Struggles

Constance engaged a broker to try to sell her business, and there were some potential purchasers who showed interest, but none of them were experienced in dealing with or trying to sell lace and were fearful of trying to do so, starting with an unprofitable business. The sales effort continued but, in the meantime, Constance had to keep running her business. She participated in some presentations where she would speak to a group and then would sign copies of her lace book, "Making It With Lace." But the effort involved - the travel, the hotel rooms, the time and preparation - was significant, and the book sales were small. Constance's initial enthusiasm for lace was wearing very thin, as was her hope of extricating herself from this project for which she once had held high hopes.

Jeremy was not making things any easier for her. His interest in her, other than to criticize her, had continued to diminish, and she detected increasing signs that he was getting involved, perhaps seriously, with another woman. Constance had not lost any of her objective attractiveness, her elegant carriage, her designer clothes, and perfect coifing. But, for those who knew her well, the sparkle in her eyes was gone, and she seemed preoccupied, because she was. "Jeremy," she said, "Let's be honest. Is it all gone? Everything?"

Jeremy was curt, "I can't answer that, Constance. Is it all gone? Is there nothing left in our lives except your shop?"

"If it would do any good, I would simply acknowledge that my venture into lace, which seemed so appropriate at the time with Kate Lord's involvement, has turned out to be a mistake. But I have always thought, from the moment of our marriage, that our love and our marriage would endure in the face of whatever mistakes either of us made. I had always thought that we were a team, committed to each other, and that you could lean on me in difficult times, and I could lean on you. My love, my feeling of commitment, has remained as constant as my name. It has never flagged. Maybe I have been expecting too much of you, and maybe being too much of a trial for you, but I have felt that mutual commitment faltering. Will it help for me to say 'I'm sorry, let's reach deep within ourselves and recapture our romance? Will that help? Or must I conclude that I am consigned to 'going it alone,' regardless of whether we stay together or don't?" Constance spoke with tears and emotion as she reached out to grasp Jeremy's hand hanging at his side.

"Connie, you are putting a guilt trip on me when I felt I was the one who was abandoned, yes, abandoned to the boutique, which sapped every bit of energy and enthusiasm from you. I was working hard every day in the clinic, and you didn't care about the clinic or my work. The shop had stolen you from me. I hated that shop of yours, and - although I never hated you - I felt estranged from and abandoned by you. Is there still a path for us to rekindle the flame? Maybe, I'm really confused right now and not in a position to say anything. It's going to take some time. Give me some time, and I will try to give you some sympathy, *if* you will do whatever it takes to get rid of that damned shop. One more thing, Connie, you are still mixing pain killers with alcohol. You know that can be deadly to you in a physical sense. But it also deadens the real Connie that I married. I don't know yet how serious that problem is, but will you try to find the strength to put it behind you? You might have felt this was the only prop you had when wrestling with the shop issues, but it was a barrier between us. Can you deal with life without the drugs?" Jeremy countered.

"Jeremy, I honestly rarely mix my pain pills with alcohol. I mean that. I simply have to take something for my back pain, and once in a while I also allow myself a glass of white wine, or two, usually hours after my last pain pill. I will try to see if I can get by on over-the-counter pain relievers, so I can still have some light, white wine, with dinner. If I do that, can you be faithful to me, Jeremy?" Constance asked.

It was as though Constance had thrust a sword through Jeremy. He said, "Excuse me," and he walked away. "I'm going to bed," he said.

Constance slumped down in a chair as she heard Jeremy slamming the door into the guest bedroom. "It's gotten to be standard," Connie said quietly and slowly to herself. "I'm beginning to wonder if he's going to abandon our bedroom entirely. How do these things happen? I start out trying to bury the hatchet, be forgiving and affectionate, trying to heal a rupture, and then somehow it gets worse instead of better. He finds something about me to criticize, and then I defend myself, and I say things, and he says things that are hurtful and damaging - worse than if we hadn't tried to talk it out at all. I might have to accept that we may be nearing the tipping point if we are not already there. Is it really all about the shop? Or is there some unseen and inevitable force I can't control that's going to finish tearing us apart?"

Upstairs, in the guest bedroom, Jeremy wondered if the children were sleeping soundly. Already in his pajamas, he rose from the bed, opened the door, and peeked into the children's bedroom and looked affectionately at the softly breathing children, sleeping quietly with no awareness of the turmoil in their world. He thought, "I hope I can sleep like that tonight, but instead I'll probably toss and turn, and keep looking at the clock. I love these kids, and I don't want anything to hurt them. But I seem to have lost the ability to love their mother, and I have lost the natural instinct to try to heal the increasing rift. I even find myself resistant to Connie's peace moves. I just sort of want to leave, get away. It's visceral, illogical, and maybe petty, but we are heading for disaster, and I can't help myself. It looks like it is written somewhere in the stars that Connie and I just aren't meant for each other. I don't seem to be able to do anything about the way I feel. Well, good night, little ones. Keep on sleeping well."

CHAPTER TWENTY-FIVE: Lunch with the Professor

It was mid-morning, the shop was staffed for the day, the nanny had arrived, and Constance had a strong conviction that now was the time to have a serious talk with her father. He answered her telephone call, and his professional sounding "Hello" changed immediately to a warm and cheerful, "Hi, Connie! Great to hear from you. I know you've been busy, but I have missed talking with you, and it's great to hear your voice." Constance suggested having lunch, and he was free, so they met at the High Spirits Inn. "You know, Connie, I try to avoid calling you very much because I know how busy, sometimes even frantic, you are, but I wanted to talk with you and had planned to call you today. So, this worked out perfectly. What on your mind?" Professor Selsby asked.

"Dad, thanks for seeing me on short notice," Constance began. "I've put off calling you lately because I've been hoping I would have good news to tell you, but it hasn't happened yet. I'm still hopeful, and I'm not a quitter. You didn't raise me to be a quitter, and I am looking at the future positively as far as the lace business is concerned. Still, I wanted you to know where I am and how I see things working out, and I just felt the strong need to have someone to share my thoughts and plans with and get your thoughts and reactions. We are not making any money at the store, but we hope things will get better. The truth is, we are losing money at the moment, partly because most new startup businesses do lose money at first, and partly because Kate Lord walked out on me.

But I got a money judgment against Kate, which has helped greatly, and I developed a business relationship with this synthetic lace company in New York that put me on a retainer and pays me extra for some TV ad spots I'm doing for them. I think you know most of this, but those two sources of funding have enabled me to make ends meet - barely. I'm trying to develop a mail order business for lace kits and patterns, but it's slow and expensive. I don't know how well the Sim Lace people are doing, or how long that relationship will last. So, the future looks cloudy, but the clouds don't frighten me, and I'm not here to ask for more financial support. You have been more than generous to me, and to Jeremy, and I am going to do everything in my power to make a success of this business. I want you to be proud of me for starting a successful business."

"I've seen the ads you've 'starred' in, via the TV set, and I was proud of you. You have theatrical talent. Good job!" Selsby said.

"Actually, I have been approached by another company to do some ads for them, so maybe that's my niche, my future," Connie mentioned. "The problem is that time is not on my side. Jeremy gets increasingly resentful of the time I'm having to devote to the success of the shop, and I am very concerned that there is not enough time left for me to get the shop on a firm footing before our marriage blows up. It's bad. If we talk with each other to try to work things out, it turns out we just get into a bigger fight. And it's not just the shop. I think he has a girlfriend, probably his nurse assistant. Of course, our problems don't just affect us; we have two beautiful children who are also affected. Not only that - which is a deep, deep chasm - but Jeremy has been contributing half of the cost of our monthly mortgage pay-off and half of our repayment of the loan advance you made to us. Jeremy is not rolling in money at this time. He's still in the process of getting his pediatric practice off the ground, so child support and alimony are not going to be very generous if it comes to that. So, I am at a crossroad and don't know what is going to happen next. I have this sense of being lost and lonely. First, it was Kate Lord; then it has been my own husband,

Jeremy; and my social friends aren't supporting me in my shop the way I thought they would. I feel so alone in all this. I needed to share it with you, knowing you will never abandon me and might have some words of advice or encouragement."

"You are right, Connie," her dad assured her. "I will never abandon you. You know how much I love you. But I do need to share with you a big development in my life. That's one reason I was glad you called, and that we got to have this lunch. Now, hold your breath: I might be getting married again! Okay, I can see the shock. It's someone I met on a cruise, and her name is Margaret Perkins, but she calls herself 'Maggie.' She lives in the horse belt of Virginia, in a large house. She is widowed, husband had cancer and died several years ago. She has two grown children, a son and a daughter. The son is supposedly a banker in the Midwest, unmarried, and the daughter lives in Washington, D.C., married with one child, a daughter, who teaches in a private school. Maggie is a lot of fun, great conversationalist, and she is an avid reader - seems knowledgeable about everything. She likes to travel and has traveled extensively. She also knows a lot about horses. I'm planning to have her come down here so you can meet her and so that she can see where I live. We would probably spend a part of each year in Virginia and part in Carolina. Now, do you think you can stand up under the shock of all this?"

Connie stumbled and struggled to recover her composure. "Dad, how old is this person?"

"She's three years younger than I am, seventy-one. She's very attractive and very active," Selsby said.

"Dad, I've always wanted you to be happy. We lost Mom just at the time you would have been able to travel and do things together, without so many responsibilities of work and civic engagements. I can't say that you rushed back into the institution of marriage, but it does seem like you are rushing a bit regarding this particular person. You hear all the time about widows who go on cruises just to find a new husband, and they put on all the charm to do it. I only hope you are making the right decision, and I am comforted in knowing that you have always made very careful and deliberate decisions. I have to say I am a little concerned that you might be living a good part of the year in Virginia, because this is a time in my life when I may need your counsel more than ever," Connie managed to say.

"Connie, we have telephones, and Virginia is not very far from Greenville. I don't see any problem with communication. I'll always be available to you, and you will always be my top priority," her dad assured her.

"Is she into horses in a big way, Dad? Is she one of the horsey set?" Constance asked.

"She does have some horses, three of them, I think. One's a potential racehorse and two are show horses. I get the impression she has never had her own horse in any races, although she follows the races. She likes to have horses around, thinks they are beautiful animals. They have to be maintained, though, and it isn't cheap. But if we got married, Maggie would have her finances and I would have mine - separate books entirely. She would not have any influence over your and my finances or relationship," Selsby said reassuringly.

"When are you having her come down, Dad?" Constance asked.

"No date set yet," Selby said. "We'll have to work out the details. Now, back to the reason we got together today, you wanted my advice. I don't know that I have any great words of wisdom to offer. You have a thorny problem. You have a commercial business, not yet quite making it, but with some hope, over time. Problem is, you have domestic and financial issues that constrict your timeframe for making the business work out for you. I am not sure you wouldn't be better off just ditching it now and cutting your losses. Don't worry about the embarrassment. It would quickly pass, and you would be able to recapture your life. I've come to realize that living a life free of severe avoidable tension outweighs every success you might achieve in a cut-throat competitive world. My life has not been free of problems either. You should know that I will work with you on any debts owed to me. I'm not so sure I would let Jeremy off the hook if he is not fair with you, but you are protected, as far as any indebtedness to me."

"But I'm a fighter, Dad, and I want to honor my commitments - especially to you. You are the last person on earth I would allow to be a loser on my account," Constance protested.

"That's one of the reasons I love and respect you so much, Connie. But knowing that, and knowing the pain it would cause you to go the last mile to keep your commitments, in my book that is as good as keeping the commitments. You tried, and tried hard, and you have been hit with some unforeseeable setbacks, not your fault. Under the circumstances, you have suffered enough, and your suffering transfers to me, and I suffer. Connie, it's just money, and we'll all make it, regardless of what happens. Use your own judgment, but you see where I stand. Love has a place, indeed, the most prominent place, in all this, and you know I love you incredibly much. I am proud of you. By the way, I am impressed with the book you have published. You've shown so much talent and resourcefulness throughout this whole effort. I'm proud of you, and I would say, put it behind you, but of course it is your choice." Professor Selsby looked at his largely uneaten lunch, now having cooled off considerably, and at Connie's similar plate, and they both laughed. Selsby paid the charges, they both rose and left, and they shared a hug in the parking lot, a very long hug.

Constance went home, in something of a daze, trying to get a handle on what had just happened at lunch. Her dad had advised her to close down the shop and essentially not to worry about what was owing to him. But that all seemed to be obscured in relation to the news that he might be on the verge of remarrying. She did not feel that the potential remarriage would be a literal abandonment of her. As Professor Selsby had observed, it would be easy for Constance and him to stay in touch, so why should she care? Yet, it was a big change, possibly like the big change that might be occurring between her and Jeremy, with the children issue added. In the midst of her other circumstances, this was one more development akin to abandonment she was feeling so strongly before the meeting with her dad.

CHAPTER TWENTY-SIX: Back to the Counselor

Professor Selsby proceeded with his marriage to Margaret Perkins, with a small family-only wedding in Maggie's home in Virginia. Constance, Jeremy. and their children drove up for the nuptials. It was the first time Constance and her family had met Margaret, as her earlier planned trip to Greenville had not taken place. Margaret's daughter and sole grandchild were there, but the son was absent and was said to be "rehabilitating," supposedly due to the stress of his work. The wedding, already planned, went forward, but the honeymoon would be postponed, pending the son's medical recovery. Constance's dad greeted Constance and her family warmly, but there was little opportunity for any private conversations.

Margaret seemed almost effusively friendly, nervously moving about, and perhaps a bit too familiar, too quickly. Constance assumed the nervousness was understandably due to the son's rehab. Margaret was matronly and had an affinity for showy hats, like she was about to leave for the Kentucky Derby, Constance thought. Constance's eyes, though, were drawn to a pin on the bride's jacket worn the evening before the wedding. "That's a piece of my mother's jewelry!" Constance thought. Margaret confirmed that it was indeed jewelry that once had belonged to Constance's mother. "How could Dad do that!" she said to herself, as Margaret explained it was intended as just a little token representing the uniting of the two families. But Constance wondered if *all* of her mother's nice jewelry, which she had always assumed would one day be hers, would eventually be bestowed on this person who had been a total stranger until just now. The festivities were cut short in view of concern for the son, whose name was Charles.

Constance and family said good-bye to her dad and Margaret, as the newly-weds needed to visit Charles. The report was that Charles had an addiction problem but was about to be released from the rehab facility. Professor Selsby and Margaret had returned to her home in Virginia after checking on Charles, and it was decided Selsby would be residing in Virginia for at least some time, in view of concerns about the progress of Charles' recovery. Constance also found that she frequently had to speak first to Margaret, who tended to answer phone calls first, before speaking to her dad, and she knew Margaret would be listening to her father's end of their conversations.

Several painful months passed by for Constance as she began trying to negotiate rent reductions for the shop and settlements with other creditors. In the meantime, her relationship with Jeremy was not improving. Jeremy had been sued for medical malpractice and, although the claim was insured, the case had received a fair amount of notoriety that had damaged his professional standing and patronage. They lived in a sort of loveless détente, where they acrimoniously endured each other but could not seem to break up. Constance decided it was time to consult with Ted Born, hoping he would give her some advice how to negotiate the near future.

"Ted, I've had a lot of crossroads, and now I'm at another one," Constance began.

"Crossroads are not always so bad, Connie. The worst thing is when there are no crossroads, only dead ends. I'm glad you still have options. Tell me where you find yourself and what options you see," Ted responded.

"Maybe I misspoke, Ted. I might be closer to a dead end than to crossroads," Constance picked up on the metaphor. "Here's where I am in a nutshell. I'm working toward closure of my shop, trying to negotiate with our landlord and other creditors. I thought maybe I could hold on to the mail-order business, selling the kits by mail even if the shop closed, but the kits are so costly to put together that I lose money on each one I sell, and customers will not pay more for them, so I don't have the option to raise prices on the kits. I've been pouring money from the Kate Lord settlement and the Sim Lace retainer into the business to keep the shop doors open until the debt reduction talks get firmed up to the point we can close the shop, but we don't yet know how or when that will come about, and the money is running out. My marriage appears to be shot, and the shop might be partially responsible, but not entirely. My dad has remarried a woman whose son was an alcoholic, and has now become a drug addict too, and Dad is having to shoulder part of the trauma of that situation. By the way, Dad has been giving my mother's jewelry to this new wife of his. To top it all, I no longer seem to have any social friends; they run when they see me coming, maybe because they think I am going to try to sell them something. And, as you might imagine, I am suffering from depression. So, what roads do you see that are open to me, and which ones should I take?"

"Of course, Connie, the obvious solution is bankruptcy, as we have mentioned before, if you can't negotiate big discounts from creditors. It might not solve all your domestic problems, but it should ameliorate them, and it might help with the depression as well. There comes a time when liquidation is the best and most sensible solution, and it looks like you are headed there, one way or another," Ted offered.

"But I can't begin to tell you how all of this has devastated my pride, Ted. I set out on a mission, and I told everyone it was a mission, not just a shop. I wanted to be something, do something. I wanted to fly. When my dream is gone, a lot of my life and spirit are also gone. I understand the logic of what you are saying, and I find myself confronting the reality of having no alternative but to be a quitter. But that's not who I am. I am a competitor, a fighter. I keep hoping for a breakthrough. I keep telling myself that, if I just hang on a little longer, something will happen to help me salvage my dreams, turn everything around," Constance countered.

"Connie, sometimes the best laid plans of mice and men go awry. Sometimes, you have to accept reality that you have given an idea a fair shot and it's not working. How long have you had the shop now?" Ted asked.

"About two years, or a little more," Constance replied.

"Do you think there is something about lace that just doesn't mesh well with the times we live in? Maybe your shop would have been a great success a hundred years ago, but people are all in a hurry; they want things pronto; they don't want to go to the trouble or take the time to devote to lace and things made of lace. You have worked hard, resourcefully, and made the necessary commitment, but perhaps the concept was not tenable in today's zeitgeist. I'm not saying that is the case, because I don't know. I haven't made a study of consumer malleability and convertibility in today's world, where lace is concerned. You set out to convert people, to make them see the beauty of lace and get them to change their priorities and be willing personally to devote the time and money to create beautiful things - a tough undertaking, especially in a society where most young women, your main target market, are working outside the home as well as seeing to their households. To be successful today, it is pretty well necessary to identify a need that a lot of people have that is not being met, and then finding a way to meet it. What I'm saying is, the fault may be in the concept you had, and that really can't be cured," Ted challenged her.

"I can't argue with a lot of what you say, Ted, but it is too late to change the choice I made, and I recognize I have no decent alternatives for my business, or even my life. Maybe Kate Lord was right, and I was doomed from the beginning," Constance said.

"It might not be all bad, Connie. Take the kits, for example. There is a lot of potential in the kits because they represent a potential national market, unlike your shop that catered mainly to a limited local clientele. You say you can't get your costs down low enough to make a profit on the kits. I suspect that is because you don't have an efficient way of measuring and packing the lace into the kits. I suggest you look into finding a way to outsource the production and filling of orders for the kits. I'm confident there are companies that can do it much less expensively and more efficiently than you can do it in-house, maybe still not cheaply enough. But it is worth checking into. You could then concentrate your efforts entirely on advertising and getting orders that you pass along to your fulfillment house. That's one thing you could try that could potentially turn a money loser into a moneymaker," Ted advised.

"That's good advice, Ted. But I think it is too late, and it might not be possible to get a low enough fulfillment quote anyway. I'm thinking I should resign myself to putting the whole lace initiative behind me, and try to recoup my life outside the world of lace. I'm really tired of the struggle, Ted," Constance confessed.

"As far as your family situation is concerned, it's hard for me to give you any advice. In the first place, it is not a legal question, and, in the second place, I don't know your father at all, even though he apparently was nice enough to recommend me to you, based on word-of-mouth hearsay, I guess. And I have only had a few casual encounters with your husband Jeremy. Of course, marriage is an intimate relationship. I don't know what makes your dad tick, nor Jeremy," Ted advised.

"I really wasn't expecting advice as to how to cure the intra-family problems. I just wanted to give you a full picture of the stresses that I feel right now. I look back, and my dream was to make an esthetic impact in an upscale niche, and now I find myself cornered and essentially clueless about how to get out of it and reclaim my life," Constance reflected.

Ted smiled and said, "Connie, I know you are an authority on the Greeks and Greek mythology, actually living in a Greek-themed home, but I've heard you say you wanted to fly. Not many people would express it that way. But it reminds me of Pegasus, the winged horse who had a connection with Mt. Helicon in Greece."

"I do know that mythology, Ted, and it's similar to the one about Icarus. His father, who was said to have been a renowned sculptor and creative genius, gave Icarus a pair of wings made out of wax and feathers, but warned Icarus not to fly too close to the sun because the wax wings might melt. Icarus ignored his father's warning and tried anyway to fly close to the sun. The wings melted, and that was the end of Icarus. Maybe I am a small-time Icarus," Constance sighed.

CHAPTER TWENTY-SEVEN: A Call from Vinnie

The telephone rang, and Constance answered it with the cheery voice she had cultivated in striving for good customer relations. But it was not a customer this time. It was Vincent Bocelli from Slim Lace. "Hi, Connie. This is Vinnie. How are things going down your way?"

"Well, Vinnie, this is a complicated business, and I have come to realize that art - which is what lace is all about - doesn't mesh easily with normal business. You inspire me because you have found a way to make a mass market out of an artistic product. Being in a kind of partnership with you has broadened my horizons, and I hope has been helpful to you as well," Constance responded.

"Yeah, well, Connie, you've been a great asset to us. Your ad spots have given some class to our products, and we have no doubt they have been very helpful in our sales. You've certainly earned every penny of the retainer we've been paying and the extras for the ad spots - three of them, I think, as of this point," Vinnie offered.

"I appreciate your saying that Vinnie. I have learned a lot from you, and I hope I've done my part to further your sales efforts," Constance said.

"Yes! That's one thing I was calling about. As a startup company ourselves, we've stumbled some and struggled, and we have been trying to run this company in our spare time, as Maury and I both are hanging onto our regular jobs. We haven't been able to find the right manager, so, as I indicated, it hasn't been such smooth sailing - although I think we've made good progress. Anyway, we've been talking up the business among our contacts, and someone has come out of the woodwork and wants to buy our company. Maury and I both think it would be good to do that - pocket a little profit and move on. So, we're hoping that, within maybe 60 days, we can close the deal. Now, Connie, we don't know how this is going to affect you, as we don't control that. They might have their own business plan that's entirely different from ours. When we close the sale, unless the new owner directs us otherwise, we will have to deliver to them the company with as few strings attached as possible, so they can step in and do their own thing. So, we will honor our contract with you, but we will have to terminate it as of the date the deal closes. So, you will be guaranteed all compensation owing to you under our mutual agreement, but after that, it's all really up to the new owners. I would guess they will come visit you to see if and how you and their company can march along together. But I just wanted you to know what's going on. We are supposed to freeze all discretionary spending - and that includes you, except for our existing contract with you - until the closing. That's the usual way, because they and their lawyers will be doing what they call 'due diligence,' and they understandably don't want any ground shaking under them while they are doing that. We certainly thank you for your help and wish you the best," thus Vinnie broke the news to Constance that there was a new ballgame in town.

Vinnie had been diplomatic and complimentary to Constance, but the best way she could interpret the message was that the contractual retainer and ad spot income was probably about to end on its upcoming expiration date. She gathered herself together enough to ask Vinnie who the new purchaser was and what kind of company they were. Vinnie responded guardedly, "Connie, we've been pledged to secrecy about this deal. They told me I could speak to you about the fact your relationship would be under review, but they do not want us to identify them. I can say that it is a good-sized company with a distribution system and customer contacts in place, which they think will enable them to hit the ground running and vastly expand sales. But that's all I can tell you now. At some point before closing, they might authorize me to tell you more, or they might wish to tell you themselves as a part of their due diligence, and they may want to interview you."

"Okay, Vinnie. Thanks for being straight with me. If I can see my way to help the new owners, I'll be happy to cooperate. Let's stay in touch. Bye," Constance said.

Constance had hoped that, even after her shop closed, she could still earn personal income by doing ad spots for Sim Lace or its new owners, giving her a modest source of income, and maybe get asked to do TV spots for others. It would be a new career that could give her a lot of flexibility in her time and greatly enhance the possibility for a good home life. Now it looked like that was probably not going to happen.

CHAPTER TWENTY-EIGHT:
An Evening at Helicon Heights

Constance closed the shop at the end of the day and drove home, depressed by the message she had gotten from Vincent Bocelli earlier that day. She tried to sort out where she could go from there, assuming the likelihood that any linkage with Sim Lace would soon be at an end. Jeremy was not there, probably seeing his girlfriend, Constance thought. The children were playing in the adjacent room, and they waved at Constance but continued with their toys. She greeted the nanny, asked her if this was her payday, and was reminded that it was indeed. She began writing a check, and the nanny, Julia, said, "Mrs. Stanfield, if you have a minute, can I speak with you privately?"

"Of course, Julia. Let's step into the study and close the door," Constance said.

"Mrs. Stanfield, I like my job as a nanny, and I love your children, but you and Dr. Stanfield are so busy and are not around very much - and I understand that, please don't take it as a criticism - but I pick up on things the children say and do and what their feelings are. Well, I thought I would share some of their impressions, not wanting to make any trouble, but just thinking you ought to know. Remy came to me today and said, 'Nanny, are you our real mama?' I said, 'Oh, no, Remy, you know your real mama is at work. She works very hard for you because she wants good things for you and Angela, but you see her in the evenings when she comes home and on weekends. She loves you and Angela very much. I'm just helping her out, like a friend, seeing that you and Angela eat good meals and learn your alphabet and have fun.' And Remy said, 'I love you, Nanny. Mama never has time. She usually takes some pills and fixes something to drink, and then she lies down on the bed or on the sofa and tells us to go along and play by ourselves. Then she puts us to bed. And most of the time we go to bed before Daddy comes home. I wish . . .' and then his voice trailed off and he said, 'never mind.' Angela has said some things like that also, but, while Remy seemed sad, Angela is showing some resentment, almost anger. I know that we are all caught up in things and are often prisoners of our circumstances, and there might not be anything you can do about it, but I just wanted you to know. Maybe you could do something special with the children that would mean a lot to them. Believe me, I am doing my best to be a good advocate for you and Dr. Stanfield, and I do everything I can to praise you and tell them how proud they should be to have such amazing parents. I don't think it is a crisis, and I'm not wanting to be an alarmist. They are great kids - wonderful kids, in fact. But I think part of my job is to let you know when I pick up on their feelings. They are still so young, but I don't want you to miss any more of this stage of their development than you must. I know you want them to continue to be loving and well-adjusted as they grow. Okay, I hope I haven't gone beyond my proper role, just couldn't help myself. Forgive me if I have sounded like I was giving you unsolicited advice that goes beyond my assigned duties. I'm just an observant messenger who cares."

Constance was speechless at first. It was not something she expected to hear and certainly not something she had wanted to hear. She realized that she herself had been sensing the same sort of thing but had been telling herself, "This is just a temporary situation. As soon as we get over the hump and things start working out the way I planned, I'll make up for the lost time with the children. We will all have to look to the future and sacrifice today, and things will be better." She did not know what to say to the nanny, except,

"Thank you, Julia. That's not something I wanted to hear, of course, but I guess I need to. I'll try to plan some activities and outings so I can do more things with them. Maybe that will help. Yes, I do come in tired, sometimes mentally and physically exhausted, and I have a bad back that is painful. I'm afraid I've given priority to my own feelings and have just expected the children to adapt, hoping that, if they have been active during the day, they would not need as much attention in the evening. I realize now that things have to change. You are priceless, Julia, and I thank you for caring enough to be honest with me. Thank you, and have a good evening," Constance told her, trying to hold back the tears, feeling a crushing sense of guilt.

Constance wanted her pills and a drink, but she thought she should go check on the children first and see how they were doing. She found Angela trying to teach Remy how to play checkers. "May I play some checkers with you?" Constance asked. Both children looked surprised, but they acceded, provided they could finish their current game. Constance got down on the rug with them, where the checkerboard was lying, and then waited, hoping she herself could remember the rules of a game she had not played since her own childhood. The evening seemed to go all right, but for Constance, playing games with the children did not come easily. She sometimes felt she was trying to force a buddy-buddy relationship that was perhaps stilted at times. Her conscience told her it was all because she had been neglectful, had not tried hard enough in the past. She asked the children if they would like to stay up a little later, and she would read bed-time stories to them. They first reacted affirmatively, but soon showed disinterest. She then tucked them into their beds and gave them goodnight hugs and kisses.

"I've lost something. I have lost the ability to be a good and caring mother. My priority has been my shop, and I'm just not used to being a good mother. Now, where am I? I have lost most of my social friends; I have lost Kate; I have possibly lost my husband; I probably have lost my Sim Lace partnership; I'm losing my shop;

and my relationship with Dad has been weakened. Now I realize my children are also an issue for me - a terribly, terribly important one. I wanted to be an achiever in business and esthetics, and now I seem to be a failure at everything. I need the pills and a good strong drink, like Bourbon on the rocks, something more than a small glass of white wine. Maybe I can figure out things tomorrow. After a while, she went to sleep, sitting in a slumped position in a reclining chair.

At 11:35 p.m., Jeremy returned to the house and tried to rouse Constance. "Connie, wake up, and get up! You've passed out, and I need to get you into your bed."

"I don't know what happened," Connie struggled to say. "It was a bad day, and this just sneaked up on me. I apologize. I can make it to the bed." But she stumbled and was falling when Jeremy caught her.

"Connie, you're an alcoholic, and a disgrace! How I have put up with this so long, I don't know. This has got to stop. I never want the children to see you like this," Jeremy scolded.

"The children are lucky to see *you* in *any* condition. You're never here. Have you spent the evening with your nurse again? If anything would push me to drink, it's what you do. No love for any of your family. No moral support. No anything.," Constance responded shakily.

"We've got to talk, Connie. Now's not the time, I know. But we need to take out some insurance on you. If you are determined to drink yourself to death, we need some insurance to take care of the rest of us, especially the children. I don't have the money to raise the children on my own. You and your family have always had the money. I've done what I could, but I have student loans to repay, and I'm worried about that malpractice insurance case against me. I'm insured, but the reputation of my clinic could be ruined, and there is a possibility my insurance could be terminated, or the premiums jacked up. I would be stuck with two kids to bring up and no money. We need to get insurance on you. We can talk about it tomorrow."

"This was just a bad day for me, Jeremy. I'll tell you about it tomorrow. It's not going to be like this all the time. In fact, I do hope never again. Don't blow things out of proportion," she said slowly and with difficulty as she fell into her bed, still fully clothed. Jeremy turned off the light in the room and went out, quietly closing the door behind him.

Jeremy went to the guest bedroom, which more and more was becoming his own bedroom, and said to himself, "She's disgusting, but maybe some good can come of it, if I can shame her into taking out a term insurance policy for a lot of money, say a million dollars, that could set the stage for a resolution of this mess I'm in with this marriage.

CHAPTER TWENTY-NINE:
The Insurance Push

Constance strained to pull herself out of bed the next morning, pressing a hand to her head, hoping it would ease the pain of a throbbing headache, and feeling discomfort in her stomach. She drew on her bathrobe, roused the children, and went into the kitchen to prepare breakfast. Jeremy suddenly appeared at the kitchen door, fully dressed for his clinic. "Surprised to see you up, Connie," he remarked with a superior air.

"I always do what needs to be done, Jeremy. It doesn't matter how I feel. I just do what must be done. I hope you slept well after a rough time you must have had out on the town last night, or maybe in someone's apartment," Constance responded in the same derisive manner with which Jeremy had spoken to her.

Jeremy ignored the obvious suggestion of his probable infidelity and said, "Connie, you and I don't seem to have many real good opportunities to talk about serious things, but maybe we have a few minutes before the children come down to breakfast."

Constance continued scrambling the eggs and getting out the pre-cooked bacon. "Okay, go ahead. Tell me what's on your mind."

"I mentioned it to you last night, Connie, but you probably didn't hear me, or don't remember. I am very concerned that your alcoholism doesn't mesh with your pain pills, and I am concerned that you are going to overdose on them one of these days and not wake up. Connie, I have pleaded with you to control the pills and the alcohol, and especially to control mixing them together. You are female, and you are very thin, and in fact you've been losing weight lately, and small women cannot safely absorb pills and alcohol. A large man can tolerate them a little better, but you likely cannot. It's obvious that, so far, you have ignored my pleas, and, if last night is any indication, the situation and the risk are getting worse instead of better. Have you thought about what would happen to the children if you were to have a fatal overdose and leave me and the kids here, with a huge financial crisis on our hands? I could not count on any help from your dad, especially if I were ever to remarry; plus, we have a huge mortgage on this house, and there's the shop calamity to deal with. I don't think I could pay the nanny, much less school tuition and expenses for the children. If you love our children, it would be an act of love for you to take out some insurance, I think about a million dollars' worth, to make sure they are properly provided for in case anything happened to you. Of course, if you will turn things around and give up the pills and drinks, we might not need the insurance, but it would do no harm, and we would have some peace of mind. At your relatively young age and health profile, a million-dollar term life insurance policy wouldn't cost much, and it would mean a lot to the family," Jeremy proposed.

"Jeremy, I can't believe you would say that to me, essentially hoping for and encouraging your wife's death so you and some floozy could live in luxury, probably here at Helicon Heights, which I planned and designed - although I must say it's become more like 'Hellish Heights' now, the way things have gone. You forgot to mention that you would like me to prepay my funeral expenses as well. We need to cut this conversation off right now. Here come the children. We can talk further at another time if there's anything to talk about." Constance replied.

Thankfully, this was not a day she absolutely had to be at her shop, and Constance was stunned as she thought about what Jeremy had said. The more she thought of the brazen suggestion of insurance, especially in the context of Jeremy's obvious romantic attachment to someone else, the more furious she got. Then her fury began to turn into deep depression, as she reflected that she had no family or close friends with whom she could discuss Jeremy's latest bombshell. "I need to talk with Ted," she said to herself. "I know it's not a legal problem - or is it? Anyway, Ted knows the background, and he's trustworthy."

Ted answered his phone and told Constance he could talk with her for a while at that very moment, no need for an appointment to come see him. "Thank you, Ted. You know what I have been going through lately. Everything in my life seems to be going downhill. The latest news about the shop is that it looks like I will be losing my contract with Sim Lace, not immediately, but in a few months on expiration of the current one-year contract. I feared this might be something that would happen, although I had been encouraged that my ad shots had been well-received and thought there might be a chance for continuation. But the Sim Lace company is being sold to a conglomerate that has its own way of doing things, and I think it's ten-to-one that I will be out in a few months."

"I hate to hear that, Connie. It's one more obstacle that you have to deal with, after all the others you are facing. Any progress on getting someone to take over the packaging and mailing out of your kits?" Ted asked.

"I've got some leads. I'll be interviewing them soon, and maybe something will pan out, but frankly, I think it is a long shot, and, anyway, I'm not sure that or anything else would be enough to help much. But that's not the main reason I wanted to talk with you. I am beginning to fear for my life. You know, I think, that Jeremy almost certainly is involved with another woman, probably his nurse. I've almost given up on him, and I think he is hanging on to our marriage because he is afraid he will be hit hard when the malpractice suit comes to trial, and he is afraid the bad publicity will ruin his business. Also, he's worried about his relationship with the children. But now I am beginning to see how he's trying to get it all figured out."

"How's that?" Ted asked.

"He came to me with a proposal that I take out a million dollars' worth of term life insurance - not on him, but on *me*. If I did that, do you see how vulnerable that would make me to a husband living in the same house with me, who has lost all love for me? It would solve all his problems if something bad happened to me and he got all that insurance," Constance answered, with a rhetorical question inserted.

"I see," Ted said. "But tell me something. You have lived intimately with Jeremy for years now, and you must know him pretty well. Structurally, the existence of the insurance would perhaps make it tempting for a person with a potentially murderous personality to do something terrible to get the insurance. But a lot of couples, for good reasons, have bought insurance on just one of them. Do you think Jeremy is psychologically capable of murder?"

"I don't know how to answer that, Ted. A few years ago, I would have definitely said, 'no,' but times have changed, and Jeremy has changed, and he has this new girlfriend. I am gumming up the works for him, by being a live obstacle to his view of a path forward. And, Ted, I've been thinking of the 'vision' Kate Lord had of my demise, and I'm wondering whether it is possible that circumstances are inexorably rolling forward to that unthinkable conclusion. I know it's crazy, but I can't help thinking about that," Constance admitted.

"Connie, did anything in particular precipitate this insurance issue, other than your overall financial problems?" Ted asked.

"Well, yes. At least ostensibly, although I don't credit it as the real cause. I have always had a slender build, and I have been losing what little weight I had, because I just have no appetite in my circumstances. And for some reason, my back has been killing me. I've gone to the bone doctor, the orthopedist, and he says I have early degenerative arthritis. He has prescribed for me some pills he says might help with the arthritis, but he has also given me some stronger pain pills, just to make life bearable for me. I don't remember the name, but they are pretty potent, and they do give me some relief. Now, I am not an alcoholic - although Jeremy accuses me of that - but I have, throughout my adult life, except during my pregnancies, enjoyed a couple of relatively small glasses of white wine in the evenings, usually one before dinner and one with dinner. I find it difficult, with all that is going on, to give up my tradition of wine in the evening, even though I now am taking these pain pills when needed. Jeremy preaches to me, and I know he is medically correct about this, that it is dangerous to mix alcohol with my pain pills - I have some anxiety pills, too - especially in what he says is my 'emaciated' state. So, last night, I came home, and the Nanny told me the children were troubled by not seeing more of me, implying that I was neglectful, not being a good mother. She said it politely, but the guilt just came flooding over me, and I did something different after putting the children to bed. I fixed a straight Bourbon on the rocks and drank one glass, and part of another one, even though I had been taking the pills. I guess I more or less passed out on the sofa, probably as much from mental and emotional exhaustion as from the alcohol and pills. But Jeremy came home close to midnight and woke me up and chastised me verbally. I made it shakily to bed, but then he confronted me with the incident this morning, and brought up the insurance, which he said he had mentioned last night, but I don't really remember. Anyway, he said he was afraid I was unable to resist combining alcohol with the pills, accusing me also of being an alcoholic, and warned that this combination could be fatal. He went on to say that, if I was going to continue like this, and he said he didn't think I could help myself, I needed to take out this insurance policy to protect the children. I don't think it was the children who were uppermost in his mind, but he laid it on the children's welfare. He kept harping on the prospect I might pass out and never wake up and said I needed to take out the insurance. But I think that was a pretext," Constance said.

"I see. It would be hard to argue with the medical science, Connie, although I join you in your skepticism as to Jeremy's real motivation. Let me ask you: Has Jeremy ever physically abused you?" Ted asked.

"Probably not what you would call bad physical abuse. He has never hit or bruised me. But he has pushed and shoved me, and he has verbally abused me. There are times I have been afraid of him, especially after I got involved with the shop," Constance responded.

"Connie, Jeremy's admonitions about mixing the pills and alcohol may be pretextual, but in my limited knowledge I understand there is reason to be concerned, and seriously concerned, about mixing pain pills with alcohol. I suggest you go back to the orthopedist and ask if there are milder pain pills that don't react, or don't react in a life-threatening manner, that you can take, and ask if you can change your timing so that the pills and alcohol don't end up in your stomach at the same time. If the answers you get don't solve the problem, you might just have to decide to give up the alcohol. You might find that some kind of sparkling water, flavored with lemon or lime, might work for you instead of alcohol. At some point you have to make the choice of living or dying, and I know you to be a strong-willed person with tremendous determination to stick with a plan. I also wonder if some physical therapy might help your back so that you don't feel as much need for the pain pills, and maybe something like acetaminophen would work for you, although I understand liver damage can result from mixing acetaminophen with alcohol. Sometimes there are no simple answers. But you need to make whatever adjustments are medically indicated to be able to get through day by day, for your sake and the sake of your children. It will be interesting to see whether, if you can resolve the medical issues, Jeremy stops insisting on insurance. If he does, then you will know his concern for your safety was genuine. Maybe he will come back to you, and all will be good again. It can't hurt to get the medical issues fixed or at least made better," Ted advised.

"That's good advice, Ted. I'll see if there is a medical solution that works for me," Connie responded.

"Let me know how everything goes, and take care of yourself," Ted told her.

CHAPTER THIRTY:
Reality Intrudes

Constance went back to the orthopedist who listened patiently to her and then said, "Connie, I get this question all the time: Isn't there a way to stop my pain without requiring me to change my lifestyle? Mostly, the answer is 'no'; you have to cooperate with medical science. Now you are still young, and although you do seem to have early-onset degenerative arthritis, you can probably get away with subpar compliance - for a while. But you really do need to see a physical therapist regularly, two or three times a week, and over time your bones will harden, and your muscles will strengthen, and that will relieve some, and possibly most, of your pain. If you are committed to that regimen, I can give you something milder as a pain pill. It is still preferable not to drink alcohol with it, but it is less harmful and definitely less lethal than what you have been taking. I would still recommend trying to limit your alcohol intake to one five-ounce glass of white wine and try not to take the pain pill at the same time as you consume the alcohol. Is that a lifestyle you can commit to?"

"I guess so. I've never been a gym freak; it never seemed very ladylike, but my circumstances are making me reconsider a lot of things. Can you recommend a therapist?" Constance asked.

"I can not only recommend one, but I will write you a prescription so that for the first little while your therapy sessions will be free to you, covered by insurance, the doctor answered, writing out a prescription and handing Constance a card with a physical therapist's contact information on it.

Constance left the orthopedist's office and headed straight for the therapist. It all seemed like a strange world to Constance, looking at the treadmills, elliptical machines, rowing machines, torso rotations, and all the other equipment of which she had no conception. The therapist assured her that her x-rays and other medical records would be reviewed, and a program would be developed customized to her needs, and she would start very gradually so as to do no harm.

Constance next stopped by the pharmacy and got her new prescription filled. Then she went home to Helicon Heights. As she drove up the long driveway to the top, Constance was thinking how she loved this place that she had mostly designed over the shell of a preexisting building. "I really do want things to work out so I can live here most of my life and see my children grow up. If things don't work out with Jeremy, I'll still have the children, and I'll still have Helicon Heights. As for the shop, I can live very well without it; I no longer am going to let it define my life and my worth as a human being." She hugged the children as she came in and told Julia the nanny that she could leave for the day, and then she visited with the children and told them she expected to be seeing a lot more of them from then on.

Constance had decided to let the shop go, and just needed to find the right way to wind it down. First, she called her dad, who was still in Virginia. New wife Margaret answered the phone. "Hi, Maggie! I hope you are doing well, but I'm concerned about your son Charles. Is he well?" Constance asked.

"Tragically not, Connie," Margaret replied. "He was released from rehab, and tried to go back to work, but he was told by the bank that they were going to replace him, as they could not afford the risk of a person with a drug addiction handling money and financial instruments and other data at the bank. That sent him into a downward whirlpool of depression. He got into drugs again, and he was badly beaten up by a gang when he couldn't pay his drug debts. We just got a report from the hospital last night. He is not responding well to treatment and is in a coma much of the time. I'm worried that he won't make it, or that he will never be able to function like a half-way normal person, even if he does. We are packing the car now to drive out to see him tomorrow and will probably stay at least a few days. We might have to make some really difficult decisions soon. You want to speak to your dad - quickly?"

"Please, Maggie. I'm thinking of you and will have you and Charles in my prayers," Constance replied, as Margaret got Professor Selsby on the line. "Hi, Dad," she said. "I'm so very sorry to hear that Charles has had this horrible thing happen to him. I hope he turns the corner soon and improves a lot."

"It's one of those things we could not have predicted or expected, and Maggie is just completely torn up over it. Nothing to do but try to deal with it as best we can. I think of you and the family and your shop. How's it going?" her dad asked.

"Well, Dad, I have given it all I have, and it just isn't working. As you know, Kate Lord abandoned me, and she was key to success. I had dreams of spreading the gospel of lace and bringing in lots of converts but that hasn't panned out. Would you be disappointed in me if I had to close the shop, if it came to that?" Constance asked.

"It's not a matter of being disappointed. Not every business deal works out, and I knew that when I loaned the money. But, Connie, it's a little more complicated than you might realize. I can't get into all that right now because we need to hit the road immediately to be by Charles' bedside. But I'll try to call you tomorrow," Selsby said.

The next day he called and told Constance that Charles' injuries were worse than they had thought, with a severe skull fracture, a broken neck, back injuries, a broken arm, and perhaps some abdominal injuries among other things. Charles was unconscious and nonresponsive, on life support, and his survival was highly questionable. The thugs had beaten him unmercifully but left him in a state that would make an even louder statement to other drug "customers" than death itself. Selsby told Constance that he and Margaret were committed to staying there to monitor and care for Charles until the possibility of his survival was clarified.

"But there's not much we can do except be here and wait, so I can tell you some more about the way taxes affect the loan I made on the business if it you were unable to pay the loan. I would have to consider two different tax options. First, most creditors take a bad debt deduction when they have made a business loan that cannot be repaid. If I could do that, I would get a tax benefit from the loss. The problem is, as I understand it from my tax advisers, the loan I made to you and Jeremy would not be considered business loans made in the ordinary course of business, because I do not have any ongoing business where I regularly extend credit to customers, and, of equal importance, you are my daughter. The IRS would say I made the loan to you only because you were my daughter, and the IRS would also point out that I took no collateral on the loan, which indicates it was not a genuine commercial loan. So, the IRS would contend that this loan was made with the expectation that family members might not be able to repay it, and thus, to the extent it is not repaid, it is considered a gift, not a deductible tax loss."

"If it is a gift, would that be so bad, Dad?" Constance asked.

"Well, I would probably have to file a gift tax return and either pay a gift tax or let it eat into the amount of my estate that can be given tax-free on my death. There's talk in Washington that Congress might be thinking of increasing the amount that can be inherited tax-free at death, but that is not the case at the present. I need to think this out, but possibly the gift tax would not be as big an issue as it would have been in my past," Selby explained.

"So, does that mean you can't let us out of this debt? Because, if it does, then I don't know if I can make it work to close down the shop, and I can't see a way to keep it open without destroying everything else that we own, including my sanity," Constance responded, on the verge of tears.

"Well, there is one thing we can do. I can ask you and Jeremy to sign a note to me, effectively acknowledging the amount of the unpaid balance on the loan. Then, each year, I can make a gift to you extinguishing a portion of the debt, in amounts equal to my annual exclusion - that's the maximum amount I can give to you annually tax-free. This would require some years before the debt would be totally repaid, but it would be the safe and proper way to do it. I would give you and Jeremy separate pieces of paper each year stating how much of the debt is being forgiven. Eventually all the debt would be wiped clean, and you would owe nothing. Now, maybe all that would not be necessary now; I need to discuss it with my CPA. Give me a little time to think through it. Right now, Maggie is all torn up by Charles' situation, and I need to help with that, but I will see what I can do. Is that okay, Connie?" Selsby asked.

"I think so, Daddy. But I just have one question. What if Jeremy won't cooperate? For instance, what if we have a divorce? It just might take a divorce to get my emotional life straightened out," Constance responded.

"Bear in mind, Connie, that I've been talking only about the business debt - the money I put into the shop. I haven't been thinking of the debt you owe on all the home renovations you did. I've been assuming you will continue to repay that loan. Are we on the same wavelength?" he asked for assurance.

"Yes, Daddy, that's right. I have been talking only about the loan on the shop. We will still be repaying the house loan. But I just realized what a mess this would all be if Jeremy and I did get a divorce. He might balk at committing to pay anything further on the house if the house should be awarded solely to me. This is getting complicated," Constance mused as she thought about it.

"That would be an issue the divorce Court would have to decide. But he is already a signatory to the mortgage on the house, and he doesn't have an option to avoid dealing with the loan on the house. On the shop loan, which is just in your name, the Court could well require him to keep paying, as his children would be benefited as a part of his child support. I'm sure he expected to make good on the loan when he signed the documents. At this point, when the shop closes, you will be unemployed, with no income except child support. Anyway, that's an issue for another day. Right now, Maggie and I have a life-and-death decision to deal with, relating to Charles. We can discuss the details of your situation later. I am sorry you find yourself in this present condition. I know you have done your darndest to avoid this. Got to go now. I love you," Selsby signed off.

Constance was in a daze. She had thought it would be such an easy thing to do. She thought Daddy would just embrace her and say, "don't worry about anything, and I'll take care of it." But life is complicated, and, anyway, her dad was stressed out with the tragedy confronting him and his new wife regarding Charles. And Constance had not thought through the complications of Jeremy's having to be involved in her path forward. She wanted a drink, but she held back.

CHAPTER THIRTY-ONE: The Path Forward

It was the second day of Jeremy's malpractice trial. Jeremy came home about 3:00 p.m. and sat down with a cold beer. Julia the nanny was there with the children, but Constance had not yet come home from the shop. Jeremy ignored the children, sent them off to play on their own, under the nanny's watchful eye. He just wanted to be alone, thinking. The malpractice suit had been settled, for a lot more money than Jeremy thought was proper, but he went along with the insurance counsel's recommendation that the case be settled. There had been several witnesses who had testified, including Jeremy's nurse who, Jeremy felt, had not been a positive witness for him. Unfortunately, on examination by plaintiff's counsel, it had come out that she and Jeremy had been engaged in intimate relations for some time. Jeremy well knew that Constance had strongly suspected that relationship, but now there was recorded testimony, under oath, confirming it. The trial had also involved the testimony of two other pediatricians as expert witnesses against Jeremy's handling of the patient's case, which had angered and embarrassed Jeremy to be publicly criticized by his professional peers.

The case was now over, and he could once again go on with his medical practice, subject to the possibility of an inquiry by a medical board of review. But he felt the humiliation deeply, the first time in his career when he and his medical professionalism had been publicly glaringly spotlighted in a public forum. He wondered whether his expensive malpractice insurance premiums would increase substantially, since the insurance company had paid a bundle to get rid of the case. He had second thoughts as to his own reluctance to settle the case earlier, when it could have been done quietly and less expensively.

Jeremy had been taking life one day at a time, realizing he eventually would have to confront issues on his home front as well as at his clinic, but putting off the day of reckoning. Now it appeared he would need to face some decisions about himself, Constance, and his nurse Angie, as well as his medical practice. Still, the malpractice experience had shaken him and had left him uncertain about his own future direction, and about his capability to assess his situation and to make decisions. First, he would have to decide what to say to Constance when she would be coming home from her shop. He tried to diagnose what had gone wrong in his relationship with Constance. Was it that he was jealous that she had been in the social limelight while he had been the real breadwinner in the family in a stressful but small-scale clinic? Was it Constance's focus on her shop rather than on him and the children? Was it that he just no longer liked Constance, for reasons he could not articulate to himself? He felt tied to Constance because of her presumed access to her father's money, and he liked living at Helicon Heights, which was beyond his own financial reach, and he did not want to give that up. He also loved the children. But he wondered whether he should get a new nurse or get a new wife. It was a jumble of feelings, and the beer did little to help him make sense of where he was and where he needed to go.

"I am convinced of one thing," he told himself. "Constance and I both need to take out term life insurance. Our lives are both too unstable to continue uninsured. I tried to get Constance to do this once before, but she quit drinking and doping as much and just ignored my ultimatum. But, if I tell her we *both* need insurance for the sake of the children, she might accept that as a reasonable step we ought to take. But underlying our getting insurance is the assumption that we are going to continue living together. She has never pushed for a divorce, despite my coldness to her and my infidelity. Maybe we can try to get reconciled, if only on a temporary trial basis, and see how that works out. As for Angie, I'll never feel the same about her anymore because of her unhelpful trial testimony, but I'm not sure I can get along without her in my clinic. It would be cruel to fire her suddenly, and I don't immediately have a replacement, but I can start looking for another nurse."

Jeremy heard Constance's car pull into the garage, and then Constance entered the house and saw Jeremy, still on the sofa with the nearly finished beer on a side table. "You are home early, Jeremy. What a surprise," Constance remarked.

"We settled the lawsuit this afternoon. I didn't have any patients scheduled for today, because of the lawsuit, so I came home. Nice to see what it's like here in the daytime," Jeremy responded.

"Well, I'm sure we can rustle up some dinner, and it's good to have you here. The children will be glad to have both of us here. I will go tell Julia she can leave now," Constance said.

"You know, we both live complicated lives, and we both have a lot on our minds. The lawsuit - which I don't want to talk about - was a wake-up call to re-examine where I am and where I'm going. I know the problems with your store have probably caused you to feel the same way. I've decided I want things to work out between us. I know I've been stand-offish, sometimes insensitive to your feelings, and sometimes overly critical, but I'm going to try to do better. I've noticed you are being more conservative in your drinking. I still don't know exactly what you are taking in the way of pills, but I'm hopeful the mix of pills and reduced alcohol won't be fatal, and that's a good and hopeful development," Jeremy commented.

"I'm really glad to hear that there's a chance we can recapture the relationship we once had. I have had to face the reality that my shop cannot be salvaged and that I will have to close it down.

That will eliminate something that I think has come between us and might help make things better. But I have discovered it is not such a simple thing to do. I thought Dad would be glad just to forget my debt to him on the financing he provided on the shop, and I know he is willing, but he also gave me an education on the tax ramifications of dealing with the debt. It's not so simple. Then, too, I have to deal with the lease on the shop for the remainder of the term, even though I negotiated a reduction. It would be good if I could sublease it to someone who would take it over, but I don't know if that's possible. And there are a lot of other issues, with employees and Marcie, as well as inventory and things. Looks like my deal with Sim Lace is coming to an end. As far as the pills and alcohol are concerned, I am being very conservative, under the advice of my doctor, and you aren't ever again going to see me passed out on a couch from overindulgence. Somehow, if we both do our best, we can handle what lies ahead, and we can maybe reclaim our lives - if you will just try to come home at a reasonable hour and not stay out," Constance summarized.

"Okay. I'm going to try to do my part, but let's just talk about some things we both ought to do. For one thing, we both need some term life insurance. I'm not asking you to do anything I won't do. Let's go to an insurance broker together and sign up. It's something we need to do for the children's protection. I know when I mentioned it earlier, I mentioned only that I thought *you* should get insurance, because I was worried about your overindulgence. You seem to be beyond that now, but I think it would be a darned good idea if we both went and got some, just because you never know when we might be involved in an accident. I'm proposing that you would be the beneficiary of my insurance, and vice versa. It just makes sense to have insurance because life and health are so uncertain," Jeremy said.

"I'll sleep on it, Jeremy. The idea of taking out a big insurance policy on my life, at my age, just sounds creepy. But maybe it makes sense if we both do it. I'll think about it," Constance said.

"By the way, Connie, am I welcome to come back to our bed in our bedroom?" Jeremy asked with a smile.

"The red carpet awaits you, sir," Constance responded with a twinkle.

The next day they went together to Jeremy's insurance broker, who also handled his malpractice insurance, but could handle term life policies as well. Each took out a one-million-dollar term policy on his or her respective life, naming the spouse as the beneficiary. Jeremy told the broker he would pay the premiums and to send all bills to him.

THIRTY-TWO:
Daddy

The telephone rang at 11:00 p.m. It was Margaret, Constance's new stepmother. Constance, in bed but not quite asleep yet, answered the phone. "Connie, I am so distressed, and I hate to be the bearer of tragic news, but your father has just passed away. And I am in the hospital with bruises and cuts," Maggie said.

"Maggie, I just can't believe that! What happened? Was it a car accident?" Constance asked with a stunned voice.

"Well, yes, it was a car accident, a single vehicle accident, but it wasn't careless driving. Your father apparently had a heart attack while we were driving back on another trip to see my son Charles. We were on the interstate, and suddenly he slumped over and said, 'My chest! My chest!' and gripped at his chest, took his hands off the steering wheel and was not looking at the road. It was a terrifying moment for me. The car went off the road and down a slope on the shoulder of the road and ran into some huge rocks. We were both wearing our seat belts, but it didn't do your dad any good, because the heart attack had already gotten him. I survived, just barely, I thank God, but Grantham didn't make it. And to make it even more tragic, we were going to see whether there was any hope for saving my son Charles, and I might be about to lose him too! I know what it is like to lose a father, as I lost mine at an early age, and I am sorry to bring you this terrible message, but I didn't want you to hear it from the State Troopers' office," Margaret related.

“Maggie, where is Dad’s body?” Constance struggled to ask, with a choked voice.

“A funeral operator has it. I told them I thought we’d probably cremate him, but I wanted to get your input first. I just don’t see how I can handle a funeral right now in my condition, and I don’t even know if he has a cemetery plot. Do you know?” Maggie asked.

“I’m not sure, Maggie. Mama was buried in a cemetery with some of her family members because there was an extra plot there, but I’m not sure whether there’s room for Daddy. We never talked about it. This is so sudden! And his body is so far away. I guess cremation is best. We can always bury the urn in a cemetery plot if that seems like the right thing to do. And we can have a memorial service later. Who’s going to take care of you, Maggie, while you are recovering?” Constance asked.

“My daughter is on her way here from D.C. Now the doctor has just come in the room, and I need to talk with him. I’ve got to go. I’m sorry. Bye,” Maggie said.

Constance was in a daze. Jeremy had come in late again; it had not taken him long to return to his old habits, and he was sleeping in the guest bedroom. She went in and woke him up, relaying the tragic message she had just received. Jeremy, at first exhibiting irritation at being awakened, quickly sat up in the bed. “Connie, did he have a will?” Jeremy asked.

“Jeremy, I assume he must have, but I don’t know. I have a key to his house, and I’ll go look tomorrow and talk with his CPA and banker. I don’t think he had a lawyer, but he could have hired someone just to do his will, on his CPA’s recommendation. I’ll find out, but, frankly, I’m so torn up and in shock at his death, I haven’t even thought about whether he had a will. I just am so confused about him and his marriage to this woman Maggie, whom we scarcely know, and I am not sure how all the legal issues are going to unwind. First thing, do we just let him be cremated, which seems to be Maggie's preference?" Constance asked, partly just thinking out loud.

"Cremation would be the simplest, with all that's going on. You might not have a lot of choice. I've heard the surviving spouse has the right to make that decision. At least she had the decency to ask you. But, with the body being somewhere in the Midwest, Maggie in the hospital, and the son Charles probably dying as well, it's best just to let her have him cremated. She might ask us to split the bill, but let's wait and see. We need some legal counsel, because we owe your deceased dad a lot of money, and now Maggie's involved in all that. You need to go see your lawyer friend first thing tomorrow morning," Jeremy mused.

"I'll definitely do that tomorrow. I wish it was already daylight, so I could get started, but I know I need some sleep. Jeremy, can you at least tell me you're sorry about Dad?" Constance asked, with tears in her eyes.

"If it makes any difference, I'm sorry. But in the medical profession, we just think of death as a kind of routine thing. Death happens. It happens to all of us eventually. I guess it was just his time. But I don't like to see you crying. Try to get yourself together and go on to bed. We can think better if we can get some sleep. Now, I'm going to get back in bed. Good night," Jeremy said, as he turned out the bedside lamp and crawled back into the bed.

Constance ambled slowly back to their bedroom, got in bed, and cried out, "Oh, God! How did you let it happen? Life was complicated enough before this. Now, I don't know what to do, and Maggie is going to be in the middle of it. And Jeremy, as usual, is no help. Help me, O God! Come down from Olympus and stay by me at Helicon Heights!"

The next morning, Constance rose and got the children up, fixed breakfast for herself and the children, and said good-bye to Jeremy who rarely had breakfast. "Angela and Remy," she said as she reached over and patted Angela on the head, "Mama has something sad to tell you. I got a telephone call late last night, and Granddaddy's new wife, Miss Maggie, told me she and Granddaddy had been in a bad car accident, and she was hurt very badly, and Granddaddy - well, Granddaddy was hurt really, really bad, and he didn't make it. So, we won't be seeing him again. He's gone to be with the angels. He will look down on us, and he will be proud of the two of you, and he will want you to be good and grow up into wonderful people. But we will miss him, and we just need to be the kind of people that Granddaddy would be proud of. I don't want you to worry about it, because he's in a better place, but you can be proud that you had such a fine and wonderful Granddaddy who loved you so dearly."

The children listened quietly as they took occasional bites of breakfast, looking intently at their mother. "Mama, we are so glad we have you. Please don't cry. We'll be good." Remy added, "Yes, Mama, we promise to be good, and maybe something will happen, and Granddaddy will come back one of these days."

Constance knew she would never forget those moments at the breakfast table. Then she called her store manager Marcie to make sure the shop would be covered that morning. Julia the nanny arrived, and Constance told her briefly what had happened. Next, Constance called Ted Born's office and asked if she could come in to see him, and she was told he could see her at about 1:30 p.m. Having the morning free before her appointment with Born, she found her key to her dad's home and went there to see if she could find a will, a subject she and her dad had never discussed. She checked everywhere she could think to look, but she found no will.

At Ted Born's office, Constance was ushered in, given a cup of coffee, and she related to Ted the telephone call from Margaret. "Ted, I need some guidance. Things are in such a mess. We owed Dad for money advanced on our mortgage, as well as for my shop. Dad and I had talked about forgiveness of the loan on the shop, so

I could shut it down, but he explained there could be tax problems that might complicate it, and he would need to look into those issues. Of course, now he's married to Maggie, and I don't know how she fits into the inheritance - or our indebtedness to Dad. I don't know much about Dad's finances. I don't think he had life insurance. I think he once had a term life policy but dropped it after Mother died, as I was an adult and married and seemed not to be in great need. He was a very private person, and I hesitated to ask him about his money, because I did not want him to think I was just waiting for him to die so I could inherit his assets. What should I do, and where do I start?"

"Constance, first of all, let me offer my condolences to you," Ted gestured with his arms open. "Professor Selsby was a pillar of the community, and he was a very fine person. He will be greatly missed not only by you but by so many in the area who held him in high regard. I think you should continue to look for the will, as well as his home deed, financial papers, pensions, bank accounts, and brokerage accounts. However, the will might not be a big issue, whether he had one or never got around to making one. The reason is that, in South Carolina, your dad's re-marriage would likely have revoked any pre-existing will, which means he probably would be considered as having died intestate, even if he had a will. Where there is only one child, the widow and the child would inherit equal parts. This would not apply to any jointly held property with right of survivorship that had been executed before his remarriage, but I gather from what you've said, that he probably had no such joint property. But check it out. For all we know, he could have executed documents naming you as the sole beneficiary, such as a brokerage account or bank account, or even giving a charity a partial interest - not likely, but possible."

"I don't think there is any jointly held property. He would have surely shared that with me, and I would have likely been the one he would have chosen as a joint holder. But let's get to Maggie.

How in the world do we deal with her involvement?" Constance asked.

"I was going to say that you should look for a will, but don't knock yourself out looking for one, because even if one exists, it would have essentially been revoked when your dad married Maggie. Unless he wrote a new will *after* his re-marriage, South Carolina law is going to consider that he died intestate. That means you and Maggie would inherit equal shares of his estate. That's assuming South Carolina law applies. In the unlikely case he is deemed to have changed his residence to Virginia, then Virginia law would govern, and - if my recollection is correct -Maggie would probably get just one-third of his estate in that case. But he lived here, in South Carolina, essentially his entire life, almost certainly was registered to vote here, and owned a home here - his only home. But Maggie will almost certainly never argue he became a Virginia citizen, because she would inherit less if he were, according to my recollection of Virginia law," Born advised.

"How does that work, then, as far as our indebtedness to Dad is concerned?" asked Constance.

"Just imagine that you paid his estate back tomorrow, which would mean that the estate's liquid distributable assets would increase by that amount, in a sense canceling an IOU and replacing it with cash. It would not change the value of his overall estate because the promissory notes you signed were assets, and you would have just replaced one asset with another more liquid asset. If you inherit half of his estate and Maggie gets the other half, then you would share in half of the cash you put in to retire the debt, and Maggie would get the other half. The net effect is that, through your inheritance you would get a 50% discount on your indebtedness, but the other 50% has to be paid so that Maggie can get that as part of her inheritance. Do you know whether your dad had the right under the loan documents to call for immediate repayment at any time? That would be typical in an intra-family loan situation," Ted inquired.

"I don't know for sure," Constance replied. "Jeremy has always assumed Dad had that right, but of course Dad wasn't going to exercise that right in a way that would surprise or hurt us. Could Maggie make us repay the loans immediately?"

"Probably not immediately. First, an administratrix or personal representative would have to be appointed, and you are the logical one to serve in that capacity, since you live here where his estate would be probated and Maggie doesn't, and you are probably much more familiar with his assets than Maggie. But, in a way, you have a conflict of interest serving as the one in charge of his estate and being indebted to the estate. At some point before the assets of his estate are distributed, the loans would have to be repaid, unless Maggie agreed to accept a promissory note from you for half the debt, which I doubt is going to happen. Of course, all indebtedness of your father, if there is any, would also have to be paid out of his estate before any distribution to heirs," Ted advised.

"How long would it take for the estate to be distributed to heirs?" Constance asked.

"It depends on the complexity of the estate. Your job as administratrix, assuming the Court appoints you, is to gather together the assets of your dad's estate and see to the payment of his debts, and then, with the approval of the Probate Court, to 'settle' the estate by distributing its net assets to those entitled to their respective portions. But you will have to get appointed first, and then you will have to notify creditors to file any claims they may have, and you will have to prepare his house to be sold and maybe an estate sale of personal property. My guess is that 12 to 18 months is a good estimate. I would go ahead now and contact his bankers, CPAs, brokers, and others to get a feel for the size of his estate and whether there are any liens. Some of the people you need to talk with might not be willing to discuss his finances with you until the Court issues Letters of Administration to you, but they probably will, since you are his only child and the people you will be contacting will know you and know of your father's death. So, I suspect they will open up to you. In the meantime, assuming you are hiring me to do this, we will proceed to prepare the paperwork for getting you the Letters of Administration," Ted advised.

"Okay. I'll get started on this assignment. I've always thought Dad was worth several million dollars, but he's never shown me any financial documents, and we never discussed it. I am almost afraid to find out, although I guess I will get a substantial net distribution, which would enable me and my family to get a load of debt off our shoulders. But, of course, I would rather have Dad and continue to be under the gun financially, than to lose him and come out financially sound. Thanks, Ted," Constance, said as she shook hands with Ted and departed.

She went back home to Helicon Heights and made appointments to see some key people the next day who might shed some light on her dad's financial affairs.

CHAPTER THIRTY-THREE: The Habit

First, Constance went to Phil Blanchard, who had long been Professor Selsby's CPA, who offered his condolences to Constance. "I suppose you want to be getting into your dad's tax and accounting papers, and I know you will be entitled to them sooner or later, although he gave me strict orders not to share with you, Jeremy, or anyone else anything about his finances. I have to ask you a delicate question, though. Did you know anything about the habits your dad developed - no, it's nothing sexual?"

Constance looked blank and said, "No, I have no idea what you're referring to. What do you mean?"

Blanchard looked down hesitantly, and then looked up slowly and said, "Your dad began developing a serious gambling habit several years ago, not only on horses and sports but wild speculation on stocks - and you know, I'm sure, how the stock market has sunk, even for good stocks. Unfortunately, he was on balance a bad gambler, but he kept on with it, thinking someday his luck would turn and he would win back his losings. That's how all gamblers think. And, at the same time, he wasn't about to stop the expensive cruises he was taking. So, he dissipated a lot of his wealth. I'm not sure how much. The stockbrokers can help you on that. Personally, I think one of the reasons he married Maggie was for security. She could share expenses with him, and he could live in her house from time to time. And she was a horse lover, but smart enough not to make foolish bets on the ponies. Unfortunately, your dad had begun to bet heavily on all sorts of things. As far as I know, any bets Maggie placed were small, but they did have this common interest in cruises and horses."

"Phil, I find that impossible to believe. My dad was a straight-arrow, conservative, sensible man. He believed in living within his means, and he kept preaching that to me. What happened?" Constance asked, aghast.

"Sometimes things just snap in a person. They get dissatisfied with their lives, or they think they have earned the right to do something wild, cultivate a new set of high-roller friends, show how clever they are. I know he would never have wanted you to suspect any of that, and it made it easier to cover up and keep it from you while he was living in Virginia. I think he always believed he would end up a winner. He was convinced he was too smart to be a loser. You know, a little hubris can destroy you. And in my opinion the tension he developed, from the impact of the losses he incurred, might have contributed to his heart attack. Did you know he mortgaged his home to raise money to feed his speculative appetite, even after he had lost so much of his liquidity?" Blanchard volunteered.

"Oh, No! Not his house. That was sacred - untouchable! Not his house!" Constance fairly screamed.

Blanchard just said, "I'm sorry."

"Do you have documents that show all of this?" Constance asked.

"Well, I have his bank statements and documents I needed to prepare his tax returns, and I have some monthly statements from his stock brokerage firm," Blanchard answered. "I can't provide them to you now, but you are welcome to see them once you get your Letters of Administration papers. Of course, I had conversations with Grantham, and he pledged me to extremely strict secrecy, but he did tell me about his speculating. I should correct something I implied earlier. He didn't always lose; he occasionally won, and this would encourage him that he was on a winning streak, and then he would incur more losses. He tended to speculate big, too. Intellectually, he knew the odds were against him, but he had so much confidence he could outsmart the system, that he just kept on, sometimes increasing the size of his bets and investment stakes in terribly risky startup companies, in the hope he would win big and make up for his past losses. Unfortunately, it didn't work out that way."

"Are you saying that, at the end, he was totally broke?" Constance asked.

"I can't say that, because I don't know what his house would sell for, or what he could get for personal property at an estate sale. Of course, he might have had assets I don't even know about, although, if he did, they were not income-producing. I have the impression that, at the end, he was living mainly off his social security and a pension he got from the University. You can talk with his stockbroker and see if he still had any stocks or bonds left that were not pledged or margined or subject to some kind of lien. And check his files to see if he had any interests in timberlands or other real estate that I am not aware of. If so, it would have to be something dormant or held for future use that did not affect his income taxes; otherwise, I would know about it," Blanchard commented.

"Thank you, Mr. Blanchard," Constance said as she rose to leave. "I have to tell you that what I learned today from you has been devastating. It was so unlike the father I knew. And, of course, it turns my world upside down, because I and my family have debts that we thought we could repay with the inheritance, and I'm learning there probably isn't going to be one."

"Don't give up yet," Blanchard advised. "Do your investigation - due diligence, as they call it - and you might find a little light somewhere, though I doubt there's going to be any great windfall."

A stunned Constance left Blanchard's office. She had an afternoon appointment with the stockbroker, Harry Grimes, but there was time for her to go back to her father's house first. She went straight for the study where her dad spent so much time each day, practically living there. She found checkbooks and copies of bank statements and tax returns. The checkbook balances and bank statements seemed to confirm what Blanchard had told her. There was a metal container that could be opened only via a combination lock. Constance tried her dad's birthday and her own birthdate to see if they would open the box, but no luck. Then she tried her deceased mother's birthday unsuccessfully. Finally, she tried her parents' wedding anniversary, and that worked! Constance was gratified that her father apparently so treasured his marriage to Constance's mother that he used that numerical date to seal what he considered important items. She found the original of the deed to her dad's house, and the notes and mortgages he held on Constance's house. "Of course," Constance told herself, "I'm sure the mortgages were recorded in the Courthouse, so there's probably no way for Jeremy and me to discard them and pretend there was no loan or any mortgage, and of course his bank statements would show our periodic payments to him. Bad thought anyway, it wouldn't be right to take advantage of his death that way." She found some old term life insurance policies which obviously had long ago expired. And she found her mother's engagement ring and wedding band. There were also a couple of letters between her parents, predating their marriage, which seemed so personal that she decided not to open them, at least not yet. That was all she found in the box, but she wondered about her mother's jewelry and hoped her dad had not given it all to the new wife. She checked around in the study and in the bedroom, and she found a few pieces, but some important and expensive pieces were not found. However, she found a key to a safe deposit box at the bank and wondered what might be in it, possibly some of the missing jewelry, she hoped. She realized the safe deposit box could not be opened until Letters of Administration were issued, but she made a mental note that it should not be overlooked.

She would need to be at the stockbroker's office, about half an hour away, an hour hence, and she wondered if there was anything unspoiled and edible in her dad's refrigerator. She found a jar of three-bean salad, some red beets in the main part of the refrigerator, and some frozen breakfast sandwiches in the freezer, very adequate for a quick lunch.

Her meeting with the stockbroker went about as she expected and feared. Her dad's once robust portfolio had shrunk to almost nothing, and the remaining stocks were subject to possible margin calls because he had borrowed against them. Some of them did have modest gains in excess of the loan balances, but most were near the margins. Harry Grimes, the stockbroker, said he regretted Grantham Selsby's gambling and speculation, but he said he recognized that it was her dad's business and not his, so he just carried out transactions as directed. There might be a few thousand dollars of value left in the portfolio, provided the stock market did not go into deeper decline anytime soon and wipe out what little equity remained.

As she had seen the gist of the bank statements in the CPA's office earlier, she did not feel it necessary to go to the bank immediately, even though the most recent bank statements had not yet been delivered to the CPA, as tax season was still months away. She went home to brood about the surprising and disastrous discoveries she had made. She was faced with a first mortgage to the bank on Helicon Heights and a second mortgage held by her father's estate, plus the loan and mortgage owing to her dad's estate given to finance the opening of her shop. The shop would have to be closed and creditors paid off, in addition to the mortgage loan in favor of her dad's estate. She was unemployed, or would be as soon as the shop closed, and indeed she had not paid herself any salary for months. Jeremy had his small pediatric clinic, but it seemed fairly stagnant, perhaps hurt financially by the recently settled malpractice suit. Anyway, their marriage seemed on the rocks again. Jeremy had held onto his nurse, despite his promise to terminate her employment, and he was back to his old habit of staying late "at the office," evening after evening. He also continued sleeping in the guest bedroom at night. With her marriage threatened, no alternative income, a failed business, oodles of debt, no family to fall back on, Constance could see only a bleak future.

She had a couple of glasses of wine, realized her back was killing her again, and decided she simply had to take a pain pill - one of the really strong ones that she had retained in her medicine cabinet but had not been using for a long time. Then she left a note for Jeremy and went to bed early. Jeremy arrived late after Constance was already asleep and woke her up. "What the hell is the meaning of this note you left me, saying there's no inheritance and we are destitute!"

Constance roused herself to say, "I couldn't believe it either, but I saw the proof in the CPA's office and the stockbroker's office and in his study. Daddy gambled and speculated away essentially his entire wealth, secretly, and has been living mainly on Social Security and his pension. That's it. He talked about possible tax consequences if he forgave our debts, but estate and gift taxes were moot issues in his financial condition; maybe that was just an excuse to delay or avoid opening up to me about his true financial condition. There's no fallback, no rescue for us, that I can see. That's why I went to bed. I had as big a dose of reality as I could take for one day. I'm hoping, if I wake up in the morning, that there will be a miracle solution. It couldn't be any worse. And the worse thing of all is that it looks like I'm losing you."

"Cut the theatrics, Constance! There's something missing, or you're holding back something. We both know your dad. He was not a gambler or a speculator. Something here just doesn't compute," Jeremy said. "I guess it's no use trying to talk to you tonight. Go on back to sleep. We'll talk some more tomorrow."

"Tomorrow? We are always going to talk 'tomorrow.' But we either never talk or never resolve anything. I don't know that tomorrow will ever come or that I can accept tomorrow's reality if it comes knocking on my bedroom door. But it can't be any worse than today. Good night," Constance said as she rolled over and tried to go back to sleep.

CHAPTER THIRTY-FOUR: Another Tomorrow

A few weeks later, Constance parked her car and trudged up the steps to Ted Born's office. She had no appointment, but hoped she could see him. He was in and asked his secretary to reschedule his other appointments.

"Ted, I've just come back from New York. I've told people I went up there to talk with the Sim Lace management. I did call them, and they told me that they were about to close the deal on the sale of the company, which was as I expected. But that is not why I went to New York. *I went there to die,*" Constance said.

"You went there *to die*? What are you talking about, Connie?" Ted Born got up from his chair and leaned over his desk looking at Constance.

Constance began, "I went there to have myself killed. It was all pre-arranged. Some big brute was to break into my room and kill me, supposed to look like a burglary or something. The insurance on my life would pay off the debts and help the children grow up and have a good life. There seemed no other way. I sat there on the couch in my hotel room, waiting for the guy to come in. I was so nervous I was literally insane. What kept coming into my mind was the farewell I had spent with Angela and Remy. They gave me hugs as I told them I had to go away for a while, and they might not see me for a long time. They didn't seem to take it in. It was like, 'Well, Mama's going on another trip. So what?' I mean, I birthed these two children. They are of my own blood, the only real family I have any more, and they don't understand, and how could they possibly understand? The lacy clothes I dressed them in no longer meant anything to them or to me, only their faces, ready to face each day with hope, not knowing the grownup trauma surrounding them. But, somehow, I had to break myself away from them, hurry to the airport, and fly to New York. I made a couple of telephone calls and began waiting. The guy came into my unlocked door, had some tools with him and pried loose the chain on the door to make it look like a break-in. Then he started throwing things around to make it look like there had been a fight or a scuffle. Then he showed me a blunt instrument he could use to bash out my brains, or I could choose to be suffocated by a pillow, and he could use a rope to be sure it worked. He wanted to be paid in advance. I got out the money and handed it to him, and I told him just to keep it and go away. I just couldn't go through with it. The faces of little Angela and Remy kept flashing in my mind, and I wondered if they would remember me, and I wondered if I had been the kind of mother I ought to have been. I just couldn't go through with it. So, I paid him off, and flew back to Greenville, and I have decided to face it - to face whatever happens, as long as I am there for Angela and Remy."

Ted was so taken aback that he was nearly speechless with shock, "Connie, thank goodness you made that decision. You are right. It would have been tragic for the children, and for everyone who knows and loves you for who you are, the dreamer of maybe impossible dreams you've worked so hard to bring to reality. We admire you tremendously for that, even when the dreams haven't come to fullness the way you had hoped and planned and worked."

Constance continued, "Ted, I know what I have strongly suspected, and now I have proof, that Jeremy is in an intimate relationship with his nurse. I want to write a will and make sure nothing I have goes to him. I do have a half interest in Helicon Heights, and it is not a survivorship situation. There should be a fair amount of equity in the house over and above the first and second mortgages on it. There might be some inheritance from my father's estate. I'm going to see about removing Jeremy as a beneficiary under the insurance policy we recently took out and put it in a trust for the children. I don't want him to have anything that's mine."

Ted replied, "This is Tuesday. We should be able to get this done by tomorrow or Thursday at the latest. And how are you going to confront the multitude of financial issues you've outlined to me earlier, with the disappointment in your inheritance?"

Constance replied, "Ted, I want to live, and as long as there is life, there's hope. I'll get a job. I might even need some welfare help for a while, but I'm not going to run from it anymore. I'm going to face whatever the future throws at me. And I'm going to try to keep my pride and not be cowed by my circumstances. I will have Angela and Remy to remind me to stay on track. I haven't been regular at church for some years now, but a hymn keeps coming back to me from earlier years: 'O God, our help in ages past, our hope for years to come. Be Thou our guide while life shall last, and our eternal home.' I'm leaving here and going to the church to pray. I don't know anything else to do right now."

In the meanwhile, Jeremy was on the phone with his insurance broker. "Hey, look, Sydney. Connie and I have decided we can't really afford two insurance policies for each of us, and we don't think we really need them. Could you please cancel the policy on my life, and let's just go with the one on Connie's life?" Jeremy asked.

"Sure, we can do that. Consider it done. We'll return to you any unearned portion of your premium," the agent assured him.

"Good enough," said Jeremy.

Jeremy then called a lawyer friend of his, the one who had represented him in the malpractice lawsuit. "Hi, Claiborne. Glad we got that malpractice case settled. You and I both know I was innocent, but sometimes it's better to settle and get it behind us. Claiborne, I've got something else I want you to do for me and Connie. She doesn't have a will, and she is going through a period of stress right now, and it would really help her feelings to have a will. Could you just draw up a real simple will, nothing too complicated, just saying she's leaving everything to me?"

Claiborne responded, "I could do that, Jeremy, but it would be customary for me to talk to her first. By the way, I recall your mentioning, while we were involved in the malpractice suit, that she had her own lawyer, Ted Born. Shouldn't he be doing this?"

"Claiborne, Ted's a litigator and doesn't handle wills. And it takes forever to get in to see him. This is something that needs to be done quickly, just to ease her mind and let her know everything has been taken care of. This is not something out of the ordinary. It's just the natural thing when one spouse wants to leave everything to the other spouse. We've got these two kids, see, and she's really anxious to see that there are no complications and that the legal work will go fast and smoothly in case anything should happen to her," Jeremy said.

"Okay, Jeremy, I've got to go out of town tomorrow, but the will should be ready by Friday," said Claiborne.

"That would be perfect," said Jeremy. After hanging up the phone, Jeremy said to himself, "Might take some strong persuasion with Connie. Some of her pills and alcohol should help. I'm glad she already has the pills. I would not want to be the one who prescribed them."

On Thursday of the same week, Constance came to Ted Born's office to execute the will she had requested. They reviewed it together, and Constance said, "This is exactly as I wanted it, to remove Jeremy from any involvement with my assets if anything happens to me. This is very important to me and to my peace of mind." She signed the will with the requisite formalities, thanked Ted, and left.

CHAPTER THIRTY-FIVE:
As I Lay Dying

It was Saturday evening, and Constance lay in bed, head thrashing, then settling down, with thoughts and images flooding her subconscious. She saw ghoulish figures firing questions at her and saying things to her: "Why did you take those pills, Connie? Should you have drunk all that wine and Bourbon?" She saw her mother and her first-grade teacher. Superfast images of the past rushed through her mind's eye, but there was no time to focus. It just kept running on.

The figures in the shadows motioned to her, "Come with us. We'll be your new friends. You look tired. Come our way, and we will take care of you. You've been a failure. You might as well come with us. Come with us to a land shrouded to block out the sun. You won't be trying to fly high with your wax wings that will melt and cause you to fall. It's all foolishness. All life is foolishness and vanity. Reject it and come with us. You are our kind."

And then she saw pink clouds, angels, and cherubs, and two of the cherubs looked like Angela and Remy. "Come to us," said the angels. "We will guide you to a new place where you will have no more pain, no more worries. All will be well in the Kingdom. It is a land of beautiful lace, prettier and finer than any you have ever seen, and you can teach others how to use it to make things of beauty. You have reached for the stars, and the stars have aligned themselves to receive you."

She briefly saw a brooding image of Kate Lord somewhere between the shadowy creatures and the angels, and Constance momentarily wondered why Kate was there. Why Kate at this time - of all people! But she looked again, and Kate's image was no longer there. Are our lives somehow connected, that she would be here at this special time? Then, a chorus began singing songs she had never heard, beautiful, blended tones, all in unison. "There must be resolution," she thought. "This can't go on and on. God, deliver me! I've tried and tried to fly, and I've come so close, but I didn't make it. I didn't make it! But I believe, O God, that you will rescue me in my frailties, and in my failures, considering my dreams and faith. Look to my intent, O God; please overlook my shortcomings and redeem me. I am what I am, but consider what I want to be, a handmaiden with lace, beautiful, exquisite lace. I tried! I aspired! Is there a place in heaven for such a handmaid?" And she was received by the angels.

CHAPTER THIRTY-SIX:
To Helicon Heights

Ted Born drove to Helicon Heights after getting the message that Constance had passed away, with his wife to follow after church. The large living room had trays of food and opened bottles of wine spread on tables here and there. There seemed to be an inordinate amount of laughter permeating the scene, much like a noisy party. There were eight or ten visitors present. Ted approached Jeremy, and said, "Jeremy, I am so very sorry for your loss. What happened?"

"I just got up this morning, went to her room to say, 'Good morning,' and I found her lifeless there in her bed," Jeremy answered. "She seems to have taken a lot of pain pills - she's been having awful back problems lately - and apparently took them on top of a few glasses of wine she had been drinking. I assume the combination is what did her in. I have repeatedly warned her not to take those pills with alcohol, but she must have felt she had to have both, and this is the consequence. I'm going to miss her."

"Where are the children?" Ted asked.

"We called the nanny, and she came and got them, taking them on an outing somewhere. They only know that Mama has gone away," Jeremy answered.

"Where did all this food come from so quickly?" Ted asked.

"Oh, my nurse picked it up on the way over here. She is very thoughtful. I already had the wine and a few other things I've set out," Jeremy explained.

"Well, Constance had just come to my office to make her will, and she executed it on Thursday. I have the will in our office safe when you are ready to probate it," Ted offered.

"Oh, we know about that will, but there's a new will she made yesterday, so you need not worry about that," Jeremy said.

"Did you say 'yesterday,' Jeremy?" Ted asked.

"Yes, it was yesterday, Saturday," Jeremy replied.

"But, Jeremy, nobody executes a will on Saturday, when many law offices are closed, and lawyers are often unavailable to be sure everything is done correctly, unless they know the testator is on her deathbed. And it is certainly unusual to execute a new will just two days after executing one. Why would she do that?" Ted asked.

"She wanted to make some changes, said she had acted in haste on the first one, and had reconsidered. She felt nervous having the Thursday version floating around when it no longer reflected what she wanted," Jeremy answered.

"Was a lawyer involved in drawing up this new will?" Ted asked.

"Yes. My lawyer drew it up. She was too embarrassed to call you. But he did not handle the execution. We had a group of friends here to serve as witnesses. I hope you are not offended, but that's the way it was. Now, if you will excuse me, there's someone here I need to speak to," said Jeremy, as he moved on.

Then Lydia arrived. Jeremy looked solemnly at her and said, "Lydia, I wonder if I have just been talking to a murderer. This is the fishiest thing I ever heard of," and he told her of his conversation with Jeremy.

"I can hardly believe it,' Lydia said. "People we know don't do things like that." She noticed there was a photograph album opened up and lying on a table. She began leafing through it, which contained mainly pictures of happy times and the smiling face of Constance. When she got to the last page, she was struck by words printed on the inside of the back cover which said, "The End."

She pointed it out to Ted, who said, "You know, that's something like what Kate said she heard in her horrible dream. It's almost more than I can take - all those smiles, optimistic expectations about the future, beautiful children, and all of that is at an end for Constance. It's a tragedy! It just shouldn't have happened! I wish I could tear out those words from the back of that album and have a reset. But life is not like that, is it? What is written is written. Strange - sounds like something Kate said about the inevitability of her dream."

"I have another question I want to ask Jeremy. I want to ask him about an autopsy," Ted said to Lydia. When he finally got Jeremy's attention again, Jeremy told him he had directed that the body be cremated, and he did not expect there would be an autopsy, which would just involve unnecessary delay.

"This whole thing smells bad," he told Lydia. "The question is, what can we do about it? I no longer have Constance as a client, so I would just be in the position of a concerned citizen, and if I go too far, I could even be sued by Jeremy for tortious interference with a family matter, or slander. Let me think about it."

When Ted later learned that there was a recent million-dollar term life insurance policy on Constance's life, with Jeremy listed as the sole beneficiary, Ted was even more concerned that Constance's passing might not have been accidental. He was even more concerned when he learned that Jeremy had paid the premium on the policy and had canceled a companion policy on his own life, of which Constance had been the beneficiary. Ted said to himself, “I think I know what might have happened. I know from Connie that Jeremy had been pressing her to take out a big term life policy, and she had been ignoring his strong insistence. Then Jeremy pretended to make up with Connie, and they would both go together to get mutual reciprocal policies. Once Jeremy got her to take out a policy, I’ll bet he then quietly went back to the insurance company and canceled his own. It was a ruse to get Connie to take out the policy.”

“But you are speculating, Ted. In Constance’s depression and confusion, and with her back pain, pills and alcohol, anything could have happened. We just don’t know for sure,” Lydia cautioned.

CHAPTER THIRTY-SEVEN: Epilogue

Born mulled over what to do. He felt an intense loyalty to Constance and was an admirer of her artistic and entrepreneurial drive. Most of all, he wanted justice, justice for Constance. But he no longer had a client, and he knew nothing directly about the circumstances of her death. He was just a witness to certain facts - very suspicious facts - but did not know all the facts, the most important of which were the immediate circumstances of her death. As to those circumstances, he knew only what Jeremy had told him. Constance had no living parents or even living siblings, and certainly her stepmother Margaret would have no interest in getting involved, especially with her present preoccupation with her son Charles' medical condition. There were only two minor children, now under their father's thumbs. In short, there were no family members in a position to pursue an in-depth inquiry into the critical facts of Constance's death.

Ted decided he would go to the local prosecutor and tell what he knew. He was referred to a detective in the department. Born recognized, going in, that detectives are very busy with all kinds of criminal cases and, while potential murder would receive some priority, it was not uncommon for the authorities to get unverifiable bits of information that went nowhere. Ted told his story to the detective, Josh Graham. Graham had his file in hand and listened intently. "The problem is," Graham began, "there is a histoy of this woman dangerously mixing alcohol with pain and anxiety pills, and potent ones at that. The autopsy report showed a lethal mixture of alcohol and pain pills in her stomach. She had a thin, frail, build and even a lesser amount of the mixture could have been fatal. We understand that she had been very depressed, apparently largely because of financial problems, and had even attempted to have a hit man kill her - and then backed out at the last minute. Dr. Stanfield had repeatedly cautioned her against mixing the pills and alcohol, and she eased off for a while but lately resumed as she sank into greater depression. We have no witnesses who will say that Dr. Stanfield force-fed the concoction to his wife, and in fact he claims to have been away from the house for much of the early evening, and his nurse confirms that. And these were Mrs. Stanfield's own personal pills that she had kept in her possession for some time, not something Dr. Stanfield prescribed for her. Now, I understand that the timing of some of the events gives rise to suspicions of foul play, but charging a respected physician with murder under these circumstances would not be warranted in my opinion. You would never get a conviction. And, yes, I do understand that the Doctor had an affair going with his nurse at the time, but extramarital affairs do not provide a sufficient basis to charge murder, even considering the other timing coincidences you mention, such as the execution of the new will. By the way, those who witnessed her execution of the new will are prepared to swear that she signed it willingly and with knowledge of its contents. I will take your information up with the District Attorney, but I doubt he will think it warrants a murder charge."

Ted thanked the detective, and just said, "I knew Mrs. Stanfield well over a period of several years, and she told me very emphatically the week before her death that she wanted to live, and that she was ready to face all the consequences of the financial reversals that had occurred. I know her as a person of determination and believe she would not have taken her own life intentionally. Her husband had every reason to want her dead - the insurance plus his affair with the nurse. I predict there will soon be a new Mrs. Stanfield."

"Mr. Born, did you ever ask Mrs. Stanfield whether her husband participated in the scheme to have someone take her life in the New York hotel?" detective Graham asked.

Ted frowned with embarrassment. "That would have been an obvious question that I normally would have and should have asked, but I was so shocked by her account of the encounter with the hit man, and so relieved that she came back alive, that everything about the details of setting up the encounter just slipped into the background. Thinking back, I would have been surprised if she could have made those arrangements by herself, without some help from someone, maybe her husband. But, on the other hand, she was so much at odds with him that she was determined to take him out of her will, and she had obviously already confirmed his infidelity before she left for New York. I guess it is possible Jeremy coerced her into making the New York effort, but it is hard to see a person with her backbone going along with it. I guess there is a grapevine of people from which she could have gotten the name of the hit man. Maybe she even got a lead out of a newspaper story. I just can't figure it," Born confessed.

"Well, that's a pretty strong indication she was suicide minded, and it tremendously weakens the case for a murder charge," said Graham.

Ted told his wife Lydia of his experience with the detective, and they both agreed that the detective likely took the easy way out, being already up to his neck with other cases he deemed more pressing and more clearcut.

Ted next approached the insurance company which already had an investigative team looking into the matter. They were far more receptive to the new information and said they would proceed with both expedition and caution. The insurance company had to be very careful because it would be courting a potentially huge lawsuit for punitive damages, even exceeding the million-dollar policy limits, if a Court found that the company had unjustifiably denied a valid claim for compensation. Ted learned later that Jeremy Stanfield had settled with the insurance company for $400,000, indicating that neither party wanted to go to Court over the claim.

The circumstances of Constance's death would remain ambiguous.

Jeremy did marry nurse Angie Tatum, fairly promptly, and after marriage lived at Helicon Heights. They undertook to continue the care and education of Angela and Remy. With the insurance settlement, Jeremy was able to pay off the mortgages and other debts relating to Helicon Heights and to the shop, which was shuttered.

Two years later, Jeremy was diagnosed with stage 4 pancreatic cancer and died shortly thereafter; he had no life insurance. Angie Tatum Stanfield undertook the upbringing of Angela and Remy.

Margaret's son Charles lingered for a few weeks with the aid of heroic measures to try to keep him alive, but inevitably the tubes and the rest of the support system were removed, and he then passed on. Margaret recovered from her injuries from the accident that took the life of Professor Selsby, and she also received her share payment from the Professor's estate. She sold her house in Virginia and moved in to live with her daughter in Washington, D.C. Jeremy had agreed she could retain the jewelry that had belonged to Constance's mother.

Kate Lord, the psychic who had claimed to have seen a vision of Constance's death, had a stroke and died on the very same evening Constance died, two lives mysteriously linked by a dark vision from which Kate had sought to remove herself.

Some of Constance's customers from her former shop knew and still appreciated fine lace, and a few of them retained a copy of Constance's book on lace, a tangible legacy of her devotion to beautiful things.

Angela and Remy, Constance's most important legacy, would recall their mother with increasingly faint but fond and proud memories as they grew older. They both had artistic bents.

About the Author

Thad Long is an author and versatile attorney, with decades of practice handling difficult trials and other matters for defendants and plaintiffs in a changing litigious environment. This most recent release, **"Death at Helicon Heights"** is the fourth of "Ted Born" Courtroom drama books, following **"The Impossible Mock Orange Trial," "The Vow: Ted Born's Last Trial," and "The Jury Has a Verdict,"** which have garnered excellent reviews for accurately depicting journeys through the anatomy of high-stakes trials, with climactic endings. **"Death at Helicon Heights"** takes the reader on a you-are-there following of Ted Born's client, Constance Stanfield, as she conceives starting a boutique store specializing in lace, with a mission to increase the public's appreciation of the esthetics of beautiful lace, but she encounters difficulties at the shop and at home that severely challenge her natural disposition to overcome obstacles and succeed. The starting point of her difficulties is a dream her associate, a self-declared psychic, has of Constance's future demise, causing a severance of the partnership and many other problems, leading to Constance's depression and a self-fulfilling prophetic ending. The novel leaves unanswered the question whether the death that occurred at Helicon Heights was murder, accidental death, or suicide..

Mr. Long took his undergraduate degree from Columbia University with a major in physics and his law degree from the University of Virginia, where he served as Comments & Projects Editor of the *Virginia Law Review* and was tapped for Order of the Coif, the Raven Society and Omicron Delta Kappa. He has consistently been listed in *Best Lawyers in America* for more than thirty years, recognizing him for his abilities in an extraordinary nine different categories of expertise. He is also an elected life member of the prestigious American Law Institute and for years served as an Adjunct Professor of Law at two university law schools. He has been honored with the Lifetime Achievement Award from Marquis' *Who's Who in America.* He has served in leadership positions with many civic and community organizations. Mr. Long is married to Carolyn Wilson Long (an author in her own right, of **"Affectionately Frances,"** which has received excellent reviews), and they have had two children, Louisa Long Stockman and Wilson Alexander Long, and have four grandchildren, Kacie Grace Long, Anne Frances Stockman, Katherine Rose Stockman, and William Henry Stockman.

www.ingramcontent.com/pod-product-compliance
Lightning Source LLC
Chambersburg PA
CBHW070833020826
48982CB00019B/1064/J

* 9 7 8 1 7 3 5 7 8 2 5 7 7 *